# A Love Affair For Life

# A Love Affair For Life

*Dear Shelia,*
*You are a permanent Blessing in my life.*
*After all those years I am thankful we are still connected!*
*Love, Honor & Blessings to you and Sam*
*Always,*
*Juanda*

## Juanda L. Green

Copyright © 2011 by Juanda L. Green.

Library of Congress Control Number:    2010917987
ISBN:          Hardcover             978-1-4568-0904-1
               Softcover             978-1-4568-0903-4
               Ebook                 978-1-4568-0905-8

All rights reserved. No part of this book may be reproduced or transmitted in any form or by any means, electronic or mechanical, including photocopying, recording, or by any information storage and retrieval system, without permission in writing from the copyright owner.

This is a work of fiction. Names, characters, places and incidents either are the product of the author's imagination or are used fictitiously, and any resemblance to any actual persons, living or dead, events, or locales is entirely coincidental.

This book was printed in the United States of America.

**To order additional copies of this book, contact:**
Xlibris Corporation
1-888-795-4274
www.Xlibris.com
Orders@Xlibris.com
88875

This book is dedicated to my loving parents,
Eardis Lee and Minnie Mae Green

Every day, I think of both of you with a smile on my face.

*We are one with God who continually renews our strength. Boundless energies are ours if we would just keep in touch with God, the source of our strength. Without communion with God, we are powerless.*

Written by Minnie M. Green

# Acknowledgements

I give all praise to the one who is worthy, Jesus the Messiah; my personal Lord and Savior. You're my Rock, You're my Fortress, You're my deliverer in you will I trust.

To my son, Michael Lawrence who was with me when I wrote the first line of this book, while on vacation in the Bahamas. What a joy and blessing it is to be your mother.

To My wonderful siblings Lawrence, Michael and LaDonna I'm so thankful that we were raised to love God and each other. God did a good thing when he matched us up for our pilgrimage on earth.

To my sister in love India Green (thanks for looking out for your sister/pastor) and love to Juanita Anderson and Demetrius Ivery.

To my nieces and nephews, Jesycha, Jovan, Lauryn, Reonna, Reggie and LaDainian I just love being your Auntie, what a joy to have you all in my life.

To my cousins who supported my ministry right from the start: Florine Gildon, Diane Johnson, Robbie Jackson and Cherie Gildon-Bowman thanks for believing in me.

To all my family: Aunts, Uncle, Cousins 1st, 2nd and 3rd in San Diego and Kansas City: what fun we have had throughout the years. I am blessed by every one of you. I love you all so very much!

To my Church Family New Visions Christian Fellowship, in Los Angeles and San Diego thanks for your continual prayers and support. May the love you have given me be multiplied unto you.

To my angels on assignment: Buffy Duvall, Tamara Valdry, Donna Reed and Pat Caudle, I thank each of you for your dedication to this project. Your writing and editorial skills were invaluable. Thanks for your commitment to see this vision come to pass. I never would have made it without you.

To my divinely sent roommate Laurie Hunter, girl you are way too many things with your multi-gifted self. Iron really does sharpen iron. Thanks for everything.

To Bishop Kenneth Ulmer, thanks for affirming, ordaining and commissioning me to go forth in ministry at a time when it wasn't popular for women to be in the pulpit.

To my spiritual mother, Dr. Minnie Claiborne, who mentored me in the gifts of the Spirit and laid hands on me releasing the ministry of New Visions. Everything is coming to pass as you have said. Love You!

A special thanks to Karen Armstrong, Joyce Goodlow, Marsha Haywood and Theraesa Rivers. I remember all of us sitting in the car after breakfast, praying for this book project. God answered our prayers. Thank you for your continual support.

To all those who encouraged me to write, thank you so much; Nick Cooper, Loring Cornish, Gwen Brown, Victoria Lowe, and to the first real writer I ever met, Dr. La Verne Tolbert thanks for your influence.

To Brenda Lee, Joan Badzik and Loretta Randle, I thank God upon every remembrance of you. I thank God for your love in my life.

To my minister gal pales: Rev. Brenda Salter McNeil, Pastor Fran Cary, I can always count on a good time of laughter with you both, Love you for real.

To Rev. (BJ) Barbara Jenkins, Rev. Millie Fisher and all the Rev. Sisters, I love being with you all of you. Thanks for the support and sweet fellowship.

And to the "greater cloud of witness" cheering me on, I'll see you all again, one glad morning.

Cover and Graphic Designer: Laurie Hunter: LHunter50 @gmail.com

Illustrator: Jessica Higgins email: *JHiggins_JMH@yahoo.com* Deviant Art account: DustyLion.deviantart.com

Contact Information:  JLGMinistries@aol.com
*www.JuandaGreenMinistries.com*

# Preface

We all have issues that we need to deal with in our emotional lives. All of us, at one time or another, have experienced feelings of inadequacy, anxiety, anger, or numbness. The adjectives are endless. Privately, we fight to keep under control the thoughts that haunt and torment, fears that paralyze, and behaviors that seem extreme.

What we consider to be our bad behavior, habits, or character flaws grew out of events, conversations, and interactions, possibly inappropriate or inadequate, that we experienced in our childhood. These life-impacting episodes took something from us—love, approval, acceptance, attention, and the feelings of emotional abandonment set in. And we haven't been right since. Man sees the behavior, calls it your fault, and then scolds, retaliates, rejects, or abandons you, and the cycle repeats. He rarely has any idea what the "fault" really is. No one knows that empty, hurt place inside you. Sometimes you don't even know yourself.

Our focus is often centered on our character weaknesses and the mistakes we've made. We carry an internal sense of inadequacy, which is reinforced as we consistently take note of our glaring deficiencies. With this focus, we become stuck and unable to successfully move through life—sometimes personally, sometimes professionally, and sometimes both. Marred, scarred, cracked, and internally damaged, we are more in touch with our faults than with our greatness. Without dealing with our own internal faults, we forfeit and even sabotage our divine potential.

What are the consequences of all this negative energy to our health, careers, families, and relationships? What must we do to be saved? How do we save our marriages, our children, and ourselves? How do we move beyond our faults and begin to live the abundant life Jesus promised?

We have all experienced life situations that were unfair and unfortunate. Since the beginning of time, man's tendency is to blame others for our plight in life. However justified we feel in assigning blame as we accuse others, it will never bring inner or external resolution. Didn't Jesus say that we have to first remove the log in our own eye before dealing with the speck in the eye of our neighbor? It is time to stop blaming, judging, gossiping, and condemning others. Behaving in this manner never leads us to peace, wisdom, joy, or healing; you will never be made whole.

In order to take this trek, you will need much courage. It will be painful as the depth of our own narcissism is exposed, but nevertheless, we must continue to surrender to the process so that we may be well spiritually and emotionally. It is time to come clean, fess up, and humble yourself.

As a spiritual life coach, I desire to see people free from emotional baggage. I have just about seen it all. People are struggling with all kinds of situations and dealing with a plethora of issues that must be addressed. The Bible tells us to "confess your faults one to another, and pray for one another that ye may be healed" (James 5:16). Without the context of a loving, trusting environment, true confession will not occur, internal flaws and faults will never be discovered, authentic prayer for each other will not go forth, and the promise of healing will never be realized.

With effective prayer, the powerful presence of God's love brings healing, because God is omniscient (all powerful) and omnipresent (all present, not bound by time). He is also kind, gracious, merciful, and faithful. Because of all his attributes, he alone is able to reconstruct a shattered, bruised, fragile, and dysfunctional soul. Without divine intervention, the mutated soul is the predominate force that fuels our distortion of God, ourselves, and others. Mind-sets, attitudes, perceptions, emotions, and motives are tainted with a subconscious virus that roots itself within the very core of our being. Our behavior often reflects the damaged core, and interpersonal interactions are either codependent, toxic, superficial, intense, or nonexistent. Spiritual and emotional immaturity are the result as we live, move, and have our being in and from these inconspicuous damaged places.

As he walked on the earth, Jesus encountered people who were blind, deaf, mute, and lame. Some had withered hands or walked bowed over. Others suffered from demonic oppression, which served to fortified low self-esteem, helplessness, and despair. Salvation, deliverance, healing, restoration, and even resurrection from the dead were accomplished as he interacted with people. Jesus was anointed by the Holy Spirit and walked out his personal mission statement to bring good tidings to the poor, heal the brokenhearted, proclaim liberty to the captives, and release those who were bound.

You may not be physically blind, deaf, mute, or lame, but are you blind to emotional conditions that have blocked your personal growth? Do you turn a deaf ear to advice that promotes spiritual and emotional well-being? Are you mute when it comes to discussing your issues? Many are lame when it comes to walking on the path of recovery and choose to live from and remain in paralyzed, withered states of low self-esteem. Also, please note that a damaged self-esteem is the underlying culprit for every addiction known to man. It's amazing how many people are living bowed over with a heavy load of guilt, shame, resentment, bitterness, and disappointment.

This book was written with the intent to lead you down a path of healing. It is my prayer that the healing power of the Lord be released as you read. I pray for the restoration and transformation in the depths of your and my soul. As we live out our short duration on earth, may our lives truly become instruments of healing rather than weapons that leave a trail of generational destruction. May the love of God dramatically change you from the inside out, as the Good Shepherd leads you to a place of peace—the place beyond your faults—the place of refuge, his love.

**May the Lord give you new visions as you read.**

"The people who sat in darkness have seen a great light, and upon those
who sat in the region and shadow of death Light has dawned."
(Matt. 4:16, NKJV).

# Chapter 1

When Eric and Cynthia walked into my office, I thought, *"What a wonderful couple!"*

They really looked like they belonged together. Cynthia was a beautiful, well-dressed professional woman carrying a Coach purse that I almost bought for myself. She looked like she had it all together. Eric was charming and just plain ole good looking. On top of that, he was a sharp dresser and had a smile that could make you melt. They were referred to me by Brenda, a former client. Cynthia noticed that Brenda was more peaceful and seemed happier overall. Brenda attributed her personal transformation to our sessions together. After seeing the transformation of her friend, Cynthia called and scheduled an appointment for she and Eric. They had recently become engaged but were having some problems in their relationship.

I noticed that both of them were extremely nervous. I introduced myself and motioned for them to have a seat on the couch. They sat far apart and barely looked at each other. Peering into her compact mirror, Cynthia was fixated on her makeup. Eric just sat there with a blank, faraway look on his face. I had seen that look many times before from people who really didn't want to be in counseling.

After sharing my educational background and how I incorporate prayer as a vital part of my counseling methodology, I asked if they had any questions about the process. They didn't. When I asked them to tell me why they decided to seek my help, right off the bat, Eric made it perfectly clear that he wasn't the one who made the appointment and was not interested in getting help. As he spoke, Cynthia was noticeably agitated and interrupted him. She then began to go over every detail as to why they needed the sessions. From then on, they began to argue back and forth. I decided not to interrupt the dialogue so that I could just listen and observe. As I listened to them argue . . . "It's your fault that this . . ." "No, it's your fault that . . ." "If you hadn't . . ." "Well, you should've . . ." They sounded like children in trouble, trying desperately to save their own hides. Neither one of them was going to back down. I wondered how many sessions it would take for them to realize their own faults. As I glanced at the clock, I noticed that fifteen minutes had swiftly passed by and Eric and Cynthia were still in the thick of it. I had to interrupt.

COACH: Eric and Cynthia, it seems that you fault each other for your relationship impasse. You both need to understand that we all have faults, and blaming each other will never bring solution. The problems hindering your relationship go deeper than you realize. During your sessions, we will discover core issues in both of you that must be addressed. As those underlying issues are revealed and healed, you will see a transformation within yourselves and a significant change in your relationship. However, in order to discover those foundational inner struggles, I have to see both of you individually. I'd like to start with you, Cynthia. Can I meet with you privately next week? Is that okay?

CYNTHIA: Just me . . . Well, okay, I guess.

*Eric was relieved. He always thought Cynthia was the one who really needed the help.*

*He was only coming to keep her from nagging him.*

COACH: Eric, I'd like to see you after I have had at least two sessions with Cynthia.

ERIC: Sure. No problem.

They left my office in awkward silence. I watched as they walked to the elevator.

Cynthia was ahead of Eric. In order to avoid being in the same elevator with Cynthia,

Eric paused at the water fountain until the coast was clear. I knew it was going to be a rough ride home.

*"Lord, bless Eric and Cynthia on this journey. I pray that they will stay on the path as you lead them to wholeness. Amen."*

# Chapter 2

"Eric, would you please slow down. You almost hit that car. You know what? You're getting on my last nerve!" As Cynthia got louder, Eric drove faster. He wasn't listening to her, and Cynthia was not going to just sit there and take his passive-aggressive behavior. She decided to take charge of the situation. At the next stoplight Cynthia calmly opened the car door and got out of the car. After slamming the door as hard as she could, Cynthia started walking home.

Eric was furious and began yelling at her, "Cynthia, get back in the car. You are such a drama queen. Cynthia, stop being so childish. This is crazy. Get back in the *car*." Cynthia ignored him and walked faster. As Eric continued to yell, he knew that she would keep ignoring him. Knowing that Cynthia would never back down, he came up with an idea to scare her straight. As she was coming up to the next driveway, Eric quickly pulled in to block her path.

"Have you lost your mind? Did you just try to hit me?"

"There you go again, making a mountain out of a molehill. No, I'm not trying to hit you. I just want you to get back in the car." Eric was at his wit's end.

Cynthia realized that she had five miles to go before she would get home. Her brand-new shoes were killing her feet, so she grudgingly gave up the fight.

"Okay, I'll get in if you slow down. I swear if you try that mess again, I'll get out at the next red light."

Eric, knowing her like he did, knew she wasn't kidding. "All right, I'll slow down. Just get in." Cynthia got in, slamming the car door with fury. They both sat in fuming silence. Not another word was spoken out loud between them, but they both had plenty to say under their breath.

Later that week, Eric and Cynthia continued to argue and didn't resolve anything, so Eric decided to stop talking altogether. To him, Cynthia was just too emotional and controlling. He secretly wished he had never asked her to marry him. And Cynthia secretly wondered whether she wanted to marry Eric at all. She loved him and had waited several years for him to decide to marry her, but now she wasn't sure if she wanted to marry him.

It had been several days and Eric still hadn't called. Cynthia called and left plenty of messages, but he didn't return her calls. That wasn't unusual behavior for him. She hated when he chose to ignore her, but had learned to just wait it out. She concluded that he was hiding in his "man cave" and would come out of hibernation sooner or later. And when he did, she would resume the discussion right where she left off.

It had been a week and still no word from Eric. Actually, Cynthia was glad Eric hadn't resurfaced just yet. Her first individual session with the coach was the next day, and just in case she came home a basket case, she didn't want Eric anywhere around.

# Chapter 3

The next morning, Cynthia could barely get out of the house. Looking at the clock, she realized she was procrastinating and was running out of time. She was going to be late to her first session. Normally, she hated being late for any event. Whether it was a business meeting, a charity luncheon, or her annual visit to the gynecologist, Cynthia was always on time. She thought people who were late were inconsiderate of other people's time. She smiled to herself as she thought about how Eric learned that he had better not be late when they were going somewhere. It took a while, but after she refused to go to several events because he was late, he finally got it and was never late again.

As she stood in her closet perusing through her thoughtfully categorized outfits and shoes, an overwhelming sense of dread consumed her. Ignoring how she felt, Cynthia picked up the pace. She couldn't wait to report Eric's behavior as they drove home after the first meeting. She wanted to make it crystal clear that Eric really needed *help!*

When Cynthia pulled into the parking structure, she was only about five minutes late. But then, she thought about the time it would take to find a parking spot and walk to the office; she determined that it would take her at least another ten minutes. Finally, she was standing at the door, knocking. Coach opened the door.

COACH: Hello, Cynthia, come on in.

When Cynthia walked into my office, she was dressed to a T. That navy blue tailored pantsuit fit her like a glove. Those Prada shoes and matching purse must have cost a small fortune, and her perfectly coifed hair looked like she just came from the beauty shop. From head to toe, she was sheer perfection. Did she dress up like that just to see little ole me?

CYNTHIA: Coach, I am so sorry. I was late. I *hate* being late. I promise this will never happen again. I understand you are extremely busy, and I want you to know that I do value your time.

COACH: Oh, don't worry about that. It just gave me time to go over my notes from our last session. Have a seat. You look like you just stepped out of *Vogue* magazine.

CYNTHIA: I have a business meeting with a very important client right after my session. I want to make a good first impression, hence the outfit. You know, how it goes.

*Knowing full well that after her session she was going home, Cynthia had just lied.*

COACH: Yes, I do understand. How have you and Eric been since our time together?

CYNTHIA: I'm okay, but I have no idea about Eric. I haven't spoken to him. I'm sure you noticed the tension between us as we left.

COACH: Actually, I noticed the tension way before you walked out.

CYNTHIA: Yes, it was pretty noticeable.

COACH: Well, that's why you're here. Tell me how you felt knowing you were coming today? Cynthia, this is a safe place to express your true feelings. Please be as honest as you can . . . but, before you answer, let's pray.

*Cynthia respectively closed her eyes and bowed her head as the coach prayed.*

COACH: Lord, be with us. We come to you for wisdom and guidance. Bless us with your presence. Send Cynthia, your love at this moment. Embrace her as she shares today. Give her insight and revelation, wisdom and strength, courage and peace in Jesus' name. Amen.

*After the prayer, Cynthia felt a sense of calmness. Who knew prayer could have such a calming effect. Even though she felt a sense of peace, she wasn't about to tell how she was really feeling as she thought about coming to her session. "No way, I can't trust anyone with my real feelings, no one seems to understand or care how I really feel," she thought to herself.*

CYNTHIA: Eric thinks I'm the only one with the problem. He always tells me that. All we've done is fight since our appointment. We argued for three days, and then he stopped calling. Since then, I haven't heard from him. Why do men always disappear when you need them the most?

*Cynthia didn't answer my question and was actually waiting for me to answer hers. She was trying to engage me in a male-bashing session, but I didn't take the bait. When she realized I refused to participate in male banter, she continued talking.*

CYNTHIA: You won't believe what happened on our way home . . .

*And then with the skill of a well-trained lawyer, Cynthia went over the story in full detail. She was ready. She made all of her well thought out points highlighting Eric's character flaws, and would have continued if I hadn't interrupted her.*

COACH: It seems you have veered off the question. I'll repeat it. How did you feel knowing you were coming today?

CYNTHIA: Oh . . . well . . . Does it matter how I felt? All that really matters is that I'm here. Besides, how I feel doesn't change anything. Nobody ever cared about my feelings before, so why should it matter now?

COACH: When was the first time you noticed that no one was paying attention to how you felt?

CYNTHIA: I don't know. I guess when I was growing up.

COACH: Well, since no one cared about how you felt, what did you do with your feelings?

CYNTHIA: I'm not really sure. I guess I just skirt over them by doing something that distracts me. I seem to get a lot of things done that way.

COACH: Oh, skirting the issue, just like you're doing now?

CYNTHIA: . . . What . . . was I doing that?

COACH: Yes, you were. When I asked you how you felt as you got ready for your session, you began talking about Eric. Let's try again. Tell me how you felt.

CYNTHIA: Okay, I guess I can try. Well, as I began to get ready, I felt . . . a sense of trepidation. You know, like when you have to go to the dentist for a root canal. It's not something you really look forward to doing but you know you have to do it anyway.

COACH: What other feelings did you experience?

CYNTHIA: I was angry that Eric didn't have to come.

COACH: What did you do with all those emotions? Really think about it.

CYNTHIA: Well . . . hmm . . . let me see, what did I do with those emotions? I guess you could say that I shut them down and turned my focus to getting here on time. My thoughts were . . . I'll tell you about Eric, and what I think he needs to do to make our relationship work.

Maybe, I can fill in some blanks for you concerning him. I know he isn't going to tell you everything.

COACH: Oh, that's okay. I think I'll let Eric speak for himself. Cynthia, we are here to talk about you. Enough about Eric, tell me how you felt.

*Cynthia seemed to be out of touch with her emotions. I thought it was the perfect time to pull out my "how to identify how your feelings chart." The chart has pictures similar to the icon faces used on e-mails to express emotions. Underneath the icon is the word that expresses the emotion depicted.*

COACH: This chart will help you identify more of your feelings. For example, look at this one. It expresses anxiousness. Can you identify with it?

CYNTHIA: Why yes, I can. I did feel anxious . . . angry, fearful, and . . .

*As Cynthia pointed to each icon, she began to see a whole gamut of emotions she had suppressed.*

COACH: Earlier, you mentioned the idea of having a root canal. That example pretty much describes exactly what I hope to accomplish in our sessions. You see, we all have decaying roots within us that need to be taken out. These root systems are diseased and can no longer be tolerated, if we want to be healthy emotionally. They cause pain, and if left unattended, can really cause great damage. When you suppress, skirt over, or block those emotions, healing will never take place.

During our sessions, we will discover some of the places in your life where you first started suppressing your feelings. As those original wounded places are identified, God is going to bring healing to those specific broken places. When a doctor treats a wound, he doesn't pour the medicine over the whole body. He goes directly to the place of infection. Or, if surgery is needed, X-rays are taken to pinpoint the exact location of the problem before using the scalpel. It's the same way with emotional issues.

Remember, when I told you and Eric that your relationship challenges go deeper than you both realize? This is exactly what I was talking about. Yes, Eric has his own roots to deal with, but for now let's concentrate on yours.

CYNTHIA: Oh . . . okay, I understand what you're saying. That is a very good analogy.

COACH: Why don't you tell me more about yourself?

CYNTHIA: Well, for the most part, I consider myself to be emotionally well adjusted. Sure, I have my issues, but they're so insignificant, nothing I can't handle. I have always been good at achieving my goals. Whatever issues I have I'll just treat them like goals to accomplish. Let's see what else can I say? Well, by the age of thirty, I had a master's degree, my own home, and a rapidly advancing career. The only thing missing was a man. I figured that once I had the love of my life, I would be completely happy. I was okay being single until the day my best friend announced her engagement. I remember the smile she had on her face as she dangled her ring finger before my eyes. It truly was a beautiful engagement ring, and I was very excited for her. But then, I found myself looking down at my naked ring finger. I felt a deep ache trapped inside me. I felt unwanted, empty, and somehow incomplete. Although I was happy for her, I secretly wondered when it was going to be my turn to be chosen and loved. Shortly after that, I met Eric. My friend Laurie was giving her husband John a birthday party and invited me. Laurie believed that she had better matchmaking skills than any online dating service. She had already matched up a few of her friends and was always on the lookout for single available men for her girlfriends. When she mentioned the possibility of introducing me to Eric, to John he wholeheartedly agreed. They were both excited when Eric and I finally met.

Once again, Laurie was right. There was instant chemistry between us. He was so different from the other guys I had dated. *"What a good catch!"* I thought. He was a successful businessman, financially stable, and on top of all that he looked so good. He was a handsome, real man with style and class, just my type. I thought to myself, *"Maybe he's the one. I sure hope he is."*

*I took notes as Cynthia talked . . . several things stood out like a sore thumb. I saw her as a classic overachiever and wondered what was the real motive behind her purpose-driven life. Not knowing what I should address first, I silently prayed for direction.*

COACH: You have certainly made some tremendous accomplishments for a person your age. You must be a very responsible and disciplined person. Were you happy with your accomplishments?

CYNTHIA: Yes, I was very happy at first, but it didn't last very long.

COACH: If you weren't happy with 90 percent of your dreams coming true, why would you believe that getting married would be the golden key to your happiness? I noticed in your paperwork that you were married before.

CYNTHIA: Yes, but I don't really count that one. I was so young and didn't know what I really wanted. Truthfully, I wasn't in love with him. I got married because I always felt so lonely.

COACH: Tell me more about the loneliness.

CYNTHIA: How do I describe it . . . I don't know if I can. I had plenty of friends, but I wanted someone who would be attentive to me. I wanted to be loved. Whenever I was alone, I felt empty inside. I hated that feeling. When I was younger, I felt that way all the time. Over time, I guess I just learned to live with it . . . Oh, my look at the time. I have gone way over the allotted time.

*Looking down at her watch, Cynthia suddenly grabbed her expensive purse and headed for the door.*

CYNTHIA: I can't be late for my meeting. I'll call you next week for my next appointment.

*Reminding clients about the time was usually what I did. Cynthia had beaten me to the punch. Yes, she's good at skirting the issue, but I'll bring up that loneliness again. She said she had learned to live with it, I think she's suppressing it. She said she'll call next week for another appointment. Oh well, let's see if she calls.*

# Chapter 4

Cynthia was literally shaking as she walked swiftly to her car. Her first meeting with the coach certainly didn't go at all as she had planned. It was evident that a sensitive nerve had been touched. It reminded her of a time when she was actually getting a root canal. The dentist, while using the drill touched a nerve that refused to be numbed by the anesthesia. The pain was so intense that Cynthia couldn't stop shaking for hours after leaving the dental office. Although she was a master at hiding her feelings, she was unable to push down the emotional pain unleashed from her session. She sat in her car for a while just to calm down.

*Why am I so angry? I wish coach had never shown me that stupid chart. Well, at least I know for sure that I'm* pissed! *I know it was my bright idea to go for counseling, but now I wish I had never called. Coach kept interrupting me . . . oh, how I hate that! And then she had to bring up my first marriage. Why on earth did she have to bring that up? We weren't even married that long. I didn't know what I wanted back then. It was destined to be a disaster. What does a twenty-one-year-old know about love anyway? I hate to admit it, but my momma always tried to get me to slow down when it came to being in love. She offered sage advice by quoting lyrics from* Diana Ross and the Supremes *song, "Can't hurry love . . . you just have to wait." But no, I would not listen, and I certainly didn't wait. He proposed after the third date, and within seven weeks I was walking down the aisle. My relatives didn't even have enough time to purchase a decent airline ticket. They all thought I was pregnant, but I wasn't. I just wanted to be in that white wedding gown before Charles changed his mind. Maybe my "I have to hurry up and get married syndrome" has something to do with one of those root issues the coach was talking about. I did like that comparison she made between healing and having a root canal but root canals are so painful. Why does healing have to be so painful?*

Cynthia needed a diversion. The distraction of choice this time would be shopping. Shopping always made her feel better. She pulled into the mall parking structure and found a perfect parking spot with ease. She could feel the adrenaline rush as she hurried for the mall entrance. She knew the location of every store—one store in particular. She turn the corner, and low and behold Nordstrom's was having their bi-yearly sale.

Cynthia headed straight for the shoes. As much as she hated to admit it, she had a shoe fetish. She had so many shoes that she dedicated one of her closets as her very own shoe boutique. After patiently examining almost every shoe on the sales rack, she finally found the perfect pair. Although she already had several pairs of black shoes, she didn't have any by this particular designer.

"That will be $375.38 with tax. You really got a good deal. These shoes are normally $550." Cynthia smiled and nodded in agreement.

"Would you like for me to put this on your Nordstrom's card?"

Cynthia answered reluctantly, "Yes, put it on my card that will be fine." Trying not to show much concern on her face, Cynthia quickly signed the credit card slip. And then she did something she had done many times before, she rationalized her purchase to the sales person. "I've been working so hard lately, I really deserve these shoes. Every now and then a girl has to treat herself to something special."

The sales lady concurred, "In my opinion, designer shoes rank second to diamonds on a girl's best friend list." Cynthia watched how the saleswoman meticulously packaged her shoes. "I just love these shoes. They must be treated with tender and loving care. My name is La Donna. I put my card inside the bag. I would love to help you again in the future." I know she can't wait to see me again. She probably just got a very nice commission. La Donna gently handed Cynthia the package. "Enjoy."

"Thank you. I will see you soon."

Cynthia drove home calculating the monetary damage done in her head. She already had an outstanding balance of $700 plus on her Nordstrom's card. And with today's purchase, the balance would be about $1,100.

That wouldn't have been too bad if that was the only credit she had. The Nordstrom card was one of six cards, and each one had at least a balance of $1,000. Eric always tried to get Cynthia to stick to her financial plan but she never did. It baffled him that Cynthia, being an accountant, couldn't stick to a budget. "At least I'm happy that I got the shoes. I saved about $200. I hope Eric doesn't notice them when I wear them, but I know he will. I have to get a grip on my spending frenzies sooner or later . . . I guess it will be later."

When Cynthia got home, she had several messages on her phone. As she listened to each one, it occurred to her that Eric still hadn't called. He usually calls after about two weeks, no matter how mad he was. She almost started to worry, until the last message. It was Eric. "Hey, Cyn, I don't know if you remembered that I would be out of town on business for a while. I got back late last night. I know we have some things to work out. I've had some time to cool off and think about our relationship. Let's make some time to see each other and talk. Call me back as soon as you get this message."

Cynthia was relieved that he called, but she was determined to wait a couple of days before returning it.

§

Exactly forty-eight hours, almost to the minute, Cynthia returned Eric's call. His voice mail message informed callers that he was on the road again and wasn't expected back for another week. While listening to his voice on the phone greeting, Cynthia thought about how much she loved hearing Eric's voice. His voice sounded as good as he looked. When they first started dating, she would play his phone messages over and over again just to hear his voice. "Eric, I 'm returning your call. I forgot you were on a business trip. I guess things are picking up for you since you're gone again. Give me a call when you get home. See you soon." It was hard for her to hang up without telling Eric that she loved him. Although she was no longer upset with him, she wanted him to think that she was. Normally, those words flowed naturally from her lips, but this time she held back. It seemed strange for her not to say, "I love you, Eric."

# Chapter 5

It had been almost two weeks, and Cynthia still hadn't called to set up her second session. She did tell the coach that she would make her appointment for the following week, but it took her about ten days to recuperate from their first meeting. Coach mentioned that when making an appointment, she should try to call at least two days ahead of the day desired. Today was Tuesday and hopefully she could get in by Thursday. Holding her breath, she called to schedule her session for 4:00 p.m. on Thursday. The receptionist checked the schedule, and Thursday was totally booked. More important than the day, Cynthia needed a 4:00 p.m. slot. She was placed on hold as the receptionist checked for that time. As luck would have it, or as God would have it, there was a cancellation for 4:00 p.m. today. Cynthia unenthusiastically made the appointment.

At 3:00 p.m., Cynthia informed her assistant that she was leaving for a doctor's appointment. Heaven forbid that anyone from work would know that she was in counseling. Cynthia always did everything in her power to avoid being the center of office gossip. The only thing they could ever say about her was she spent too much money on shoes. And yes, she was wearing her brand-new black designer shoes from Nordstrom. When her assistant asked if she would be returning after her appointment, Cynthia said nothing. She wasn't planning to come back just in case she had an emotional breakdown; she wanted to go straight home. Cynthia headed for the ladies room to give herself a once-over in the full-length mirror. She brushed her hair, powdered her face, reapplied her lip gloss, and headed for her session, looking like a model on the runway.

§

COACH: Wow! Cynthia, I just love your shoes. You certainly have a wonderful sense of style.

CYNTHIA: Thank you. Nordstrom's was having a sale, and I decided to help them get rid of some of their inventory. I got them right after my session with you. I needed something to lift my spirits.

*Coach remembered that Cynthia said she had a meeting after her session. Now she says she got the shoes right after the session. Coach suspected there was no meeting.*

COACH: Yes, I have had my share of "lift up my spirits" shopping sprees.

CYNTHIA: Yes, I know. I guess the sale was calling out my name.

*Just as that sentence was coming out of her mouth, Cynthia remembered that she told coach she had a business meeting right after her session. She was hoping coach didn't remember she had said that. But just in case coach asked, Cynthia had the answer prepared in her mind. Oh, the meeting was cancelled would suffice.*

COACH: Let's get started, shall we. I got the sense that you were getting uncomfortable during our last session. You left in such a hurry. As I recall you were talking about being lonely and how that felt. Would you like to start there?

*She thought I wouldn't remember where we had left off. She also probably didn't think I would remember that she told me she had a business meeting after our last meeting, but I'll let her slide on that one.*

CYNTHIA: Can we pray first?

*How does she remember where we left off the last time? She must have at least eleven clients a day. I was hoping I could divert the topic altogether, but at least prayer could buy me a few more minutes.*

COACH: Of course. *I wonder if this was a sincere request for prayer or a diversion.*

Father we come to you again for your divine assistance. I praise you for the plan for today's session. May your plan be accomplished as you have ordained for your daughter in Jesus' name. Amen. All right, tell me about the loneliness.

CYNTHIA: . . . Well, to be honest, I was hoping you had forgotten that.

COACH: No, it's right here in my notes. However, we don't have to start there.

CYNTHIA: Oh god . . . Thank you!

COACH: You also mentioned how responsible you were. Are you comfortable with talking about that?

CYNTHIA: Yes, I can talk about that. I've always been a very responsible person, even as a child. I did my homework, I cleaned up my room, and I was always home before the porch light came on. My mother never had to stay on me about anything. She always told me how proud she was of me. She would always say, "Good, better, best, never let it rest until your good gets better and your better gets best." Throughout my life, I used that saying as a promise to my mom that I would try very hard to always do my best. I always wanted to make her happy. I guess that's why I was so responsible. My mother died a few years ago, but I know she's looking down on me smiling.

*Tears began to well up in her eyes as she continued to talk about her mother.*

My mother was actually more like a sister to me. She was beautiful, smart, and all my friends loved to be around her. She was so much fun. She loved playing board games. Friday nights were deemed game night at our house. My mom would pop popcorn over the stove and always put lots of butter on it. As a family, we would play monopoly until . . .

COACH: Why did you feel it was your responsibility to keep her happy?

CYNTHIA: I guess it was because she had such a hard time with my dad. They would sometimes have arguments that made my mother cry. I hated to see her cry. I was a very sensitive child and would notice the sad look on her face. That look made me sad. So I did everything in my power to . . .

*Instantly, free flowing tears began to stream down her face.*

COACH: What's going on? Why the tears . . . What are you feeling?

CYNTHIA: I don't know how to describe what I'm feeling. I guess I just miss my mom.

COACH: Remember the chart I showed you last time? Try to identify how you feel right now, at this moment.

CYNTHIA: I feel sad, and I also feel . . . I feel . . . scared.

*She then began to cry uncontrollably. She wanted to run out of the office.*

I hate crying . . . I feel like if I start crying I will never stop. I am overwhelmed by these feelings and I *hate* it . . . I have to control my emotions . . . I *hate* being out of control!

*Cynthia tried desperately to gain control over her sobbing. Grabbing her purse, she pulled out her powder compact and began carefully wiping her face. Slowly but surely she composed herself. As I watched her pull herself together, I wondered where those intense emotions came from and where they had gone. Something deeper was going on.*

COACH: Cynthia, can you tell me what was going on with you just now? It seemed like you were reliving some sort of incident. Was there any situations going on in your home that you were trying to control but couldn't?

CYNTHIA: Well, yes, I guess so. As I mentioned earlier, my parents were always fighting. My father would sometimes come home very late and very drunk. He would start a fight with my mother, and I would wake up. I had to go to school the next morning . . . that happened such a long time ago and . . . I can't change it or do anything about it. All of that is in the past and that's where I want to keep it.

*I could hear fear in her voice. Her body language screamed anxiety. Although she was able to hold back the tears, her body told the story, she wasn't finished with that pain. It was still expressing itself, but she refused to let it out.*

COACH: Yes, it happened in the past, but the unresolved emotions attached to your past will show up in your present. That deep, dull ache you described last time often indicates an internalization of a painful experience. As long as those issues remain lodged in the subconscious mind, you will still reason and act from those wounded places.

CYNTHIA: I guess it's possible that my parents' constant fighting could have affected me.

COACH: Okay, we will look at those things next time. But for now let's close out in prayer.

Lord, I thank you that Cynthia is becoming aware. We come to you in this process of discovery. Protect her as you guide her to those damaged emotional roots. You promised to heal her brokenness and release her from the prison of her emotional past. I thank you for your ability to restore our souls. Let your healing love reach to the very core of her being. Thank you that you will perfect everything that concerns her.

Thank you, Lord. Amen.

CYNTHIA: Amen.

COACH: Well, Cynthia, I'm going to give you your first homework assignment. Do you have a Bible?

CYNTHIA: Yes, I do. I'm sure I can find it.

COACH: Well, when you find it, keep it handy. Most of your homework will come from the Bible itself. I want you to read Psalm 23 every day until our next meeting. Also, keep a journal of your thoughts as you read. Oh, one more thing, don't forget to pray before you start reading.

CYNTHIA: All right, I'll see you next time.

*Cynthia decided it would be best not to promise when she would make her next appointment.*

After the first session, she was literally shaking. This time, even though she had an emotional collapse in the office, she was okay. Cynthia had never considered that she needed to be healed emotionally. But as she thought of things she hadn't said but knew eventually she would, Cynthia was no longer in denial. She was emotionally wounded and needed to be healed.

# Chapter 6

The next day, Cynthia searched everywhere for her Bible. She finally found it inside the purse she took to church last year on Easter. That was the last time she had read it and that was the last time she had gone to church. With the Bible in her hand she sat in her favorite chair to begin the assignment. The warm rays of the sun beaming from the window had a profound effect on her. The tension she hadn't noticed in her body was dissipating, and she noticed it. She treasured this tranquil moment and promised herself to schedule "simple time" in her day runner. She also wrote down a list of things that she would do during those times. Looking at nature, putting fresh flowers on the table or taking a nice scenic drive on a beautiful day were things she loved. She wanted and needed to appreciate the simple things that life had to offer.

Cynthia vowed to incorporate these simple pleasures into her lifestyle; she would be able to save a lot of money if she did. Fresh flowers every week verses shoes once a month would save her hundreds of dollars. As she thought about the simple delights of life, they reminded her of the simple yet profound prayers of coach. She had never known anyone with a real prayer life or one that was effective. Cynthia bowed her head to pray before doing the assignment. "It's been such a long time since I prayed. Usually, I only pray out of sheer desperation. I wonder if God is mad at me for not praying. How do I pray? What should I say? I remember the long prayers that the deacons in my church prayed. They prayed long, loud, and hard." As kids, we used to make fun of them when we got home from church. I can't pray like that . . . maybe I'll speak to God in a simple way like coach.

"Dear God please be with me as I read your Word. I'm sorry that I haven't prayed in such a long time. I hope you forgive me for that. But I promise to talk to you more often. Lord, I ask for your help as I read your Word. Please give me guidance, strength, courage, and understanding. Amen."

Before she opened the Bible, Cynthia began to reflect on her religious upbringing. She remembered walking down the aisle responding to the invitation for salvation given by the pastor. She was only nine years old, but she loved God and wanted to be baptized. She sang in the choir and had a lot of friends; she only went to church because of them. Church was more of a social activity for kids her age, but she did learn a few things. In Sunday school, all of the students were required to memorize John 3:16.

> "For God so loved the world that He gave His only Begotten Son that whosoever believeth on Him should not perish but have everlasting life."

Although it was easy for her to memorize scripture, she didn't always understand its meaning. For instance, she did believe that God loved the world, but it was hard for her to grasp the fact that God loved her specifically. She also remembered the Baptist Training Union classes she attended on Sunday evenings. These classes were designed to help students know the different books of the Bible and how to find particular scriptures. In that class, Cynthia learned that the book of Psalms was in the middle of the Bible. She turned to chapter 23 and read out loud:

"The Lord is my shepherd; I shall not want." Umm, I still remember it. "Yea, though I walk through the valley of the shadow of death, I will fear no evil . . . For thou art with me . . . Thy rod and thy staff they comfort me," . . . Grabbing the Kleenex box, Cynthia began to cry. She read the passage over and over again, certain words began to captivate her. The words were actually sinking in. She could see from the scriptures that the Lord wanted to be active in her life. He wanted to lead and guide her, protect and comfort her, anoint her and keep her from evil. With baby steps, Cynthia was connecting with God. She could even feel God's presence. It was almost like he was standing in the room with her.

And then the phone rang, it was Eric. He wanted to come over. Cynthia wanted to keep reading but reluctantly said okay. When the doorbell rang, Cynthia held her breathe as she opened the door. Eric was standing there looking good, smelling good, and bearing gifts. Cynthia wanted to slam the door in his face but couldn't. Eric handed her a big beautiful bouquet of soft lavender roses. "Hey, Eric, come in. Wow! Thanks for the flowers. They are so lovely." They hugged, and Eric kissed her on the forehead. He always knew what to do and what to say to make Cynthia's heart melt.

"You're welcome, baby. I knew you would love them. I missed you." Every time Eric returned from a trip, Cynthia would shower him with affection, but this time she was determined not to.

"How was your trip, or should I say trips?" Eric made himself comfortable on the sofa like he planned to stay awhile. Actually, he was hoping she would ask him to spend the night.

"The trips were fine, everything went well, but all I could really think about was you. As much as I hate to admit it, I can see how counseling could really help our relationship. How are your sessions going?"

Eric was so vulnerable; Cynthia rarely saw that side of him. She felt she could really open up and tell him about her sessions. As Cynthia talked, Eric was surprised his name didn't come up. Was she finally going to stop blaming him for all their problems? He felt relieved until her next statement. "Coach gave me a homework assignment. I have to read Psalm 23. It's been so long since I've read the Bible."

As soon as Cynthia mentioned the Bible, Eric became angry and interrupted her, "The Bible! What's up with that? Coach said that she would use prayer in the sessions. She didn't say anything about having Bible study. Oh, I guess now you're going to turn into one of those spooky tongue talking Christians."

Cynthia was confused by his response and wanted to lash back. She had just experienced God in such a special way as she read the Bible. To her, Eric had violated those sacred moments. She was silent, went back to her chair, and picked up her Bible. She said nothing; Cynthia acted as if he was invisible. Eric suddenly walked toward her in a rage. Cynthia was so frighten. It triggered the memories of the fights that occurred in her home as a child. She thought he was going to hit her. She held her Bible even tighter across her chest and silently prayed. Eric reached down, snatched the Bible out of her hand, and threw it across the room. Cynthia sat there for a while stunned by Eric's behavior. It was then that Cynthia did something she had never done before. She told Eric to leave. *"Did I just ask him to leave?"* Cynthia thought she had lost her mind. But she continued, "I want to break off our relationship for a while. I think it would be best. We can still go to counseling, and after completing our sessions we can see where we are and if we should get back together."

*"I'm breaking up with him . . . what am I doing?"*

Eric was surprised by her words but thought she was just putting on an act. Eric had always thought that Cynthia should have been an actress. She was good at commanding attention. Surely this was just another one of her award-winning performances. But something was very different about this breakup. First of all, Eric lost control of his temper; he was out of line, and he knew it. He had never conducted himself like that before, at least not when Cynthia was around. Secondly, Cynthia was the one initiating the separation. Any other time if he even remotely talked about leaving her, she became the epitome of the song, "Ain't to proud to beg," and would desperately try to hold onto him for dear life. She was upset but wasn't yelling, blaming, argumentative, or defensive. She spoke calmly and rationally, made all of points as to why she wanted sometime apart. He understood how serious she was about her decision, but he didn't understand how she could be so calm.

For once Eric's good looks and the memories of great sex simply didn't matter. Cynthia had made up her mind. She had thought about time apart for a while, but never thought she could go through with it. *"Wow! I'm not hurling myself at him. I'm not holding on to him for dear life, crying and begging him to stay with me. I still feel sad, and I'm crying but I don't feel like I'm falling apart. It's strange but I feel peaceful."*

"I do love you, Eric, but I need some time. I have to do this."

"Well, go ahead. I guess I can't stop you. I didn't really want to get married anyway!"

When Eric saw that she wasn't changing her mind, he left, slamming the door behind him. This was the first time that Cynthia didn't follow after him. She let him go. She walked over to the window and watched Eric speeding down the street. Was it really over? Obsessive thoughts began flooding her mind. *"Is he going to call me when he gets home? Is he going to meet someone else? He's not good enough for me anyway. I wonder how long it will take for me to meet someone else? Maybe we will still get married . . . by the end of the year, next year . . . I don't know!"*

By this time, Cynthia had worked herself up into an emotional frenzy. She wasn't sure what hurt her most, was it Eric's comment about not wanting to marry her or him throwing her Bible across the room? She had never seen him so angry. She always thought that if she just kept loving him and being there for him, Eric would eventually change. But for the first time, Cynthia was beginning to think that she was the one who needed to change.

# Chapter 7

"I can't believe Cynthia broke up with me. Maybe coach advised her to break up with me. I wonder what they talked about. They probably spent the whole time male bashing and swapping 'my man is a jerk' stories. Isn't that what women do when there're mad at their man? Maybe they recapped the scene in *Waiting to Exhale,* when Angela Basset sets her husband's clothes on fire. That scene seems to always give women a chance to celebrate kicking their boyfriends to the curb. Maybe I'm really losing her this time."

As soon as Eric entered the house, he headed straight for the telephone. He wanted to call and see if Cynthia had somehow changed her mind. After seven rings, Cynthia still did not answer, and Eric decided not to leave a message. He couldn't wait to drill the coach about what she had said to his girl. So he called the coach and made his first appointment. He was glad there was an opening for the next day. *"Hmmm, whatever they talked about I'll handle it tomorrow. You can be sure about that!"*

§

Eric was late for his appointment. I kept my eye on the clock and wondered if he would make it. He finally arrived, and when he walked in, I had to admit this man was attractive. He was tall, dark, and extremely handsome. And with a physique like that, he obviously wasn't a stranger to the gym.

COACH: How are you, Eric? I thought you'd never make it.

Eric: Yeah, I know. I wasn't sure I would make it either. You know, how New York traffic is?

Coach: I understand, bumper to bumper most of the time. How are you and Cynthia doing?

Eric: Oh, you don't know? I'm sure you would not be surprised to know that she broke up with me. After a couple of sessions with you, she gave me the axe. What's that about?

Coach: I really don't know. What did she tell you?

Eric: She mentioned something about needing some space to deal with some childhood issues crap. I know there's more to it than that. What exactly did you two talk about?

Coach: Eric, what Cynthia and I discussed is just between us. I can say that she does have some things from her past that she has to deal with. You seem pretty upset by her decision.

Eric: Yeah, you can say that. I just didn't expect her to break off our relationship. At least now I won't have to deal with all the marriage pressure. I should be glad.

Coach: But you're not. Tell me how you really feel?

Eric: Oh, here we go. I guess now you're going to dive right in with the "how do you feel?" and "what happened in your childhood?" questions.

*Eric was on the defensive and very agitated. He was mad and didn't have any problem showing it. In order to defuse the situation, I thought it would be a good time to say a prayer.*

Coach: Why don't we pray and then you can tell me how you and Cynthia met.

*Eric bowed his head for the prayer, but did so in defiance. He looked like a spoiled little boy who didn't get his way. I noticed his attitude, but it didn't stop me from praying.*

Father, we need your guidance. Eric and Cynthia are at a crossroad in their relationship. I know that you love them both and will lead them with your wisdom. Be with Eric today as he talks. Be with me as I listen. Amen.

Okay, Eric, go ahead and tell me how you and Cynthia met.

*Eric seemed to loosen up some when he realized he didn't have to answer the "how do you feel?" question.*

ERIC: I met Cynthia four years ago at my friend's birthday party. John and his wife Laurie had always wanted to introduce us. We met at John's party, and when the introductions were made, I was already captivated by her beautiful smile. We talked for a while, and then I asked her to dance. She was a really good dancer, and we danced the night away. When the party was over, I asked if we could see each other again. Her answer, of course, was yes. As she recited her phone number, she noticed that I wasn't writing the number down. She was sure that I wouldn't remember it, but I assured her that I would. When I called the next day, she was very impressed. I've always been good at impressing the ladies with that move.

We started going out, and I enjoyed being with her. She was beautiful, smart, and sexy. I can honestly say that I wasn't looking at her as just another bed partner, I already had several. I was honest about that right up front. Cynthia didn't flinch when I told her I had friends with benefits. But she made it very clear that she would not be part of my sexual harem. I respected her for that. Over time, I let go of the others, and we began an exclusive relationship.

In the beginning, we laughed all the time, I loved being around her. We were together all the time. But after a few months, I started to feel like she was smothering me. I hate feeling like that. And then she began looking at me with this longing look in her eyes. She looked at me like I was her knight in shining armor or something. I had to remind her that I was not Prince Charming.

Then after about a year or so, she started to really put the pressure on. She kept asking me how I felt about her and bombarding me with questions about our future together. I knew that it would only be a matter of time before she brought up the subject of marriage. Of course I was right. I was not thinking about marriage and had no problem telling her. At that time, I was still trying to learn how to be with one woman at a time.

The next year, she brought up the subject of marriage again. I don't understand why we can't just live together like everybody else. I think our generation sees marriage as an outdated institution. It's just a piece of paper; it's not all that serious. Cynthia stared at me; her sensual bedroom eyes were filled with disillusionment. I hate that look, so I disappeared. I needed a few days to clear my head from the vivid image of disappointment on her face.

After about three years, I found myself slowly giving in to her request. Deep down I really did want to ask her to marry me one day, but I wanted to do it on my terms, when I was ready. Valentine's Day was right around the corner. I knew that if I didn't propose, I had better start the search for a new girlfriend. Not wanting to disappoint her on yet another Valentine's Day, I bit the bullet and proposed.

COACH: Do you feel obligated to marry her?

ERIC: No, not really. I knew that I would marry her one day. I made the decision that if I wanted to keep her smiling, it would be best to ask her sooner rather than later. Right after that, we started fighting constantly, but Cynthia just kept going full steam ahead with all the wedding plans. I didn't try to stop her. I thought, let's just get this wedding over with so we can be happy again.

COACH: Well, I guess you were relieved when she decided to put the relationship on hold.

ERIC: Yes, I was . . . in a way, but I was very surprised. She didn't even talk it over with me. She just dropped it on me like a nuclear bomb. I was convinced that her sessions with you had something to do with her decision.

COACH: I can assure you that Cynthia came up with that on her own. You know, I'm curious about why you are so upset about the time apart. I thought you wanted to marry her on your terms. It seems to me that this was your way out.

Eric: You're right about that. She just caught me off guard.

Coach: Well, our time is up. We can continue next week.

Eric: Are you going to give me an assignment like you did with Cynthia? I hope it doesn't involve reading the Bible.

Coach: No, no assignments for now. I'll see you next week, and Eric, please be on time.

Eric: Okay. I'll see you next week, and I will be on time.

*"Whew, that wasn't so bad,"* Eric thought as he walked out the door. He was relieved that the coach hadn't bombarded him with the "how do you feel about this?" and "how do you feel about that?" typical women questions. But he knew they were coming sometime in the near future. Today just wasn't the day.

# Chapter 8

It was a beautiful Saturday morning, and Cynthia's had the whole day planned. She was always inundated with deadlines, so every night she would organize her tasks for the next day. She was great with time management but without her "master plan" as she called it, something was bound to fall through the cracks. On Saturday's she had two basic rituals. During the morning hours she would clean her condo while listening to music. She could clean, dance, and sing for hours. Actually this ritual was one of her favorites. When he wasn't away on business, Eric would take Cynthia to lunch, and together they would complete her errands.

Not being with Eric on Saturdays was easy; she simply rationalized that Eric was traveling. After all, being an international business man sometimes requires long trips out of the country. However, there was only one problem with that, Eric called every day while he was away on business. In an effort to block out her thoughts of Eric, Cynthia tuned the music up and drowned herself in the lyrics of song after song. Finally, she was able to block out her thoughts of Eric. It took some time, but she did it.

But then, "that song" came on the radio. Cynthia froze, and her mind quickly resumed its thoughts back to Eric. Cynthia could no longer suppress her emotions. Like a geyser, the fear, anxiety, and sadness came to the surface. Grabbing the whole Kleenex box she cried. "That song" was the one that she and Eric first danced to when they first met. Cynthia remembered everything about that night. She wore her favorite, sexy but classy little black dress. She had on her best perfume; she called it the "big girl's, womanly perfume." She even remembered what Eric had on. He was such a sharp dresser, and his shoes were just as stylish as hers'. On top of all of that, their conversation was wonderful, and even their sense of humor matched. They both were really good dancers and when they danced, they had the attention of everyone on the dance floor.

It was impossible for Cynthia not to think of Eric when "that song" was playing. Her statement to herself, out of sight out of mind, became the opposite cliché. "Absence makes the heart grow fonder." She still couldn't believe that she had broken up with Eric. For the rest of the day, Cynthia stayed home and cried.

# Chapter 9

On Monday morning, Cynthia was eager to get to her session. She had lots to say and needed her full fifty minutes. She was running late and didn't have enough time to dress to impress. She threw on some jeans, a T-shirt, tennis shoes, and put her hair in a ponytail. She only had enough time to put on her foundation and lip gloss. For Cynthia, that slight amount of makeup was equivalent to going outside with no makeup on at all. And that was something she would *never* do. Breaking up with Eric was one thing, and now leaving the house without makeup? Cynthia wondered if she was on the verge of having a nervous breakdown.

Cynthia arrived to the counseling center with only a few minutes to spare. She took a deep breathe and began to collect her thoughts as she entered the coach's office.

COACH: Well, hello, Cynthia.

*As I looked at her, I couldn't believe my eyes. She looked an average person, like myself who only wished they could look like a model.*

CYNTHIA: Oh, Coach, I couldn't wait to see you. I broke up with Eric.

COACH: I know. He told me.

CYNTHIA: What? He came for a session? I'm shocked. I assumed that since I broke up with him he would forgo counsel.

COACH: No, he was actually here. Of course I can't tell you what he said, but I really believe he values his relationship with you.

CYNTHIA: Hum, I sure couldn't tell from the last time I saw him. He didn't take it very well when I insisted on being apart for a while. All right, let me say it before you do . . . enough about Eric. I'm here to talk about me.

COACH: You took the words right out of my mouth. Let's pray and get started.

Father, I thank you for being with us as we talk. Reveal to Cynthia the next step of her journey to wholeness. I also pray the same for Eric. May your abundant grace rest on both of them in Jesus' name. Amen.

CYNTHIA: Amen. Well, you already know that I broke up with Eric. That's so major for me. In the past, I would cling on to him for dear life at the thought of him ever leaving me. This time I was the one breaking off the relationship. That's like a miracle for me. I still felt sad. I cried, but I felt a calmness that was so amazing. I attribute that peace to the assignment you gave. Spending time with God and his Word truly made a difference in me. I'm beginning to understand that the Lord is my Shepherd for real.

COACH: Wow! Isn't it wonderful to experience peace that surpasses all understanding?

CYNTHIA: Yes, it is, and that's a perfect way to describe it.

COACH: Cynthia, I'd like to ask you a question about something you just shared. You said that in the past you would cling on to Eric at the thought of a breakup. What were you so afraid of?

CYNTHIA: Afraid? I'm really not sure.

COACH: Did you react this way in other relationship breakups?

CYNTHIA: Yes, I did all the time. I always felt like I was being abandoned. I would get a panicky sensation in my stomach. I even feel it now. Oh god, I hate this!

COACH: So, were you afraid to be alone? Or is it something else?

*As Cynthia thought about her past break ups, something significant was emerging.*

CYNTHIA: No, it wasn't that. *Cynthia began to cry uncontrollably. And yelled out,* Who's going to love me now?

*There it was, the epiphany, the moment of enlightenment. The words came blurting out. It was the desperate cry of a little girl trapped, buried beneath the rubble of an emotional earthquake to her soul. It was a desperate cry that came from a deep, distant place, a forgotten place, an abandoned place. It came from the core of a broken and bruised heart. God wants access to that place.*

COACH: Remember what I said about a doctor pouring ointment directly on the wound?

A core place is being touched. This is the place where you became captive, locked in a prison of pain. And this pain is still causing you grief. Your constant search for love is the result of this wound. It's the catalysis that fuels your loneliness, neediness, depression, and fear. The Lord promises to be near those who are brokenhearted. God wants to heal and restore that broken piece of your heart. He's standing at the door of your heart, knocking. If you are willing, he will also give you the faith to open the door. Do you want to let him in?

CYNTHIA: Yes, but I'm still scared.

COACH: That's okay. You gave the Lord permission to walk you through this. And if he brings it up, it's time to be healed. Your statement "Who's going to love me now—where did that come from? You sounded like a little girl when you said it. Whose love did you lose when you were young?"

*Even though her tears subsided, Cynthia was shaking.*

CYNTHIA: I don't know. My parents never got a divorce. Both of them were at home.

They never abandoned me.

COACH: Father God, I pray for the little girl Cynthia. Holy Spirit, I ask that you would go to that hidden place of pain within her soul. You are omnipresent, oh Lord, and you are not bound by time. You can see our past, present, and future, all at once. You know all, and you see all things regarding Cynthia. I praise you for the healing you are doing even now. You are Jehovah-Rophe, "The Lord Who Heals." You can heal all levels of man's being: spirit, soul, and body. Today, I ask for emotional healing for Cynthia. Send your grace. I pray in Jesus' name. Amen.

*As I prayed, I kept my eyes open to watch Cynthia's reactions. She looked like a little girl to me. I spoke softly, knowing that the Holy Spirit was helping her make the connection.*

COACH: Cynthia, what's going on? It seems like God is showing you something. Can you talk about it without disconnecting from what you are experiencing? I don't want you to start explaining from your head. Try to stay with what's going on in your spirit, in your heart.

CYNTHIA: Well, this is really weird. I can see a picture of myself as a child. It's a picture that was taken when I was in the first grade. I was six years old. That picture is vivid in my mind.

COACH: Tell me about the picture, and see if you can remember what was going on with you during that time.

CYNTHIA: I do remember that I was appointed good citizen of the month. This was the day of the celebration. I was holding the American flag. My hair was neatly combed in two long braids. I had on one of my favorite outfits. It was a plaid jumper dress with a pretty white blouse that had beautiful lace on it. I had on some white ankle socks and a new pair of black-and-white Buster Brown shoes. But . . . I look so sad.

*Another round of tears began flowing from Cynthia's eyes.*

COACH: Okay, what just happened? Do you remember something?

CYNTHIA: Yes, but I am so scared right now. I feel extremely nervous and scared.

I'm remembering what happened the night before . . . It's like a forgotten dream slowly coming back to my mind. But, it's not a dream. This really happened . . . and it's like I'm reliving it and I really don't want to . . . Oh god!

COACH: You are not alone, Cynthia. God is with you. The Shepherd is with you.

Yea, though you walk through the valley of shadow and death, he is with you.

*This was a hard place for Cynthia, but God was about to bind up this bruised place. I knew what God was doing, but it was hard to see her in such emotional pain. I kept praying under my breath.*

COACH: Can you tell me what's going on now?

CYNTHIA: I remember the night before the ceremony. When I went to bed, I heard some sounds coming from my parents' room. My mom was crying and my father was yelling. I got up and ran to their room. And when I opened the door, I saw my father hitting my mom. I was so scared. I was afraid that he was going to kill her. I had to do something. I tried to stop him. I pulled at him, but he pushed me aside and yelled at me. He told me to go back to bed. *Go back to bed?* How could I go back to bed? How could I sleep knowing that my mother's life was in danger? If her life is in danger, what about mine, my brothers. I ran out the room to my brothers' room down the hallway. Both of my brothers were asleep. I woke them up and got them out of bed. In the middle of the night, with our pj's on and no shoes, we ran to the house next door to get help. Our neighbors came and stopped the fight. They put us back to bed and stayed to talk to my parents. That's what happened the night before the ceremony, and that's why I look so sad. The next day, no one ever talked about what happened.

*By this time Cynthia was crying uncontrollably once again.*

Since that incident I rarely slept soundly. If I remotely heard yelling, screaming, cursing I often laid there in turmoil., crying and much afraid. Instead of being peaceful as I tried to sleep, I was tormented by fear.

COACH: Holy Spirit, Cynthia needs your touch. I ask that Jesus would rescue her and be with her in this memory. Show her your glorious presence and bring your healing love to your daughter.

*As I prayed, I noticed that Cynthia was calming down. The tears stopped and her face became serene.*

COACH: What's going on now?

CYNTHIA: Even though I have my eyes closed, I can see . . . like a video flash back of this scene in my life. It's like I'm reliving it again, but this time something is different. I can still hear the sounds, the crying and yelling. But I see a bright light entering the room. It's a radiance, like the "touched by an angel" light. I'm starting to see someone in this light. Oh my god, it's Jesus. I can't really make out the image, but I know it's him. He's right here with me . . . holding my hand . . . he's really with me . . . I must be going crazy. Is this for real? I hear him talking to me. He's saying, "I'm sorry that you had to see this, but this is the result of living in a broken world. I am healing your from this incident, and I would like for you to help others who are going through similar pain. Would you like to do that for me?" His Words are giving me peace. My answer is, "Yes, yes, Lord, I would like to help others if that's what you desire. Yes, I will."

*For the next few moments we both sat there in holy silence. God was so very present. That peace that surpasses all understanding was again prevalent. Neither of us wanted to leave that place of serenity.*

*Cynthia rested on the couch for another five minutes with her eyes still closed. She wanted to talk but could barely speak.*

CYNTHIA: Wow, that was so deep! I have never experienced anything like that before.

What was that? Unbelievable!

COACH: Don't try to understand right now. Just receive deeply in your heart. How do you feel at this moment? Don't formulate full sentences. Just give me single words and short phrases. Take your time. Don't rush this.

*Cynthia took several minutes to reply.*

CYNTHIA: I feel . . . peaceful . . . light . . . stronger and calmer. Deep within, something's different.

*Cynthia was still basking in the glory of God. Even though our time was up, I couldn't disrupt this divine moment. I left the room to make a phone call. She'll come out when she's ready. Finally Cynthia came out of the room and was able to speak again.*

CYNTHIA: Coach, for real, what was that? I could barely move, and it was like I was in another realm or dimension or somewhere. I can't explain it.

COACH: It's pretty hard to explain, but let's just say you were in the presence of God. At times, his presence can be so tangible, and when healing deep places in us, it's like "holy anesthetic" comes over you, so God can do his supernatural, spiritual surgery.

That's the best way I can explain it. When describing spiritual occurrences, words often fall short.

Remember the Humpty Dumpty nursery rhyme? Humpty Dumpty sat on a wall. Humpty Dumpty had a great fall. All the king's horses and all the king's men couldn't put Humpty together again. It seems Humpty wasn't able to get the appropriate help he needed in order to be restored. Why would anyone put a fragile egg on a wall anyway?

We have all had experiences growing up that had a "great fall" impact on us that left us in broken pieces. You fell under the impact of being raised in an alcoholic environment. Breaking up that fight was horrifying. It scared you and left you emotionally fragile. My god, you were only six years old. This crisis affected the very core of your personhood. Can you see how damaging that is? You were so scared and needed consoling, but your parents were too busy fighting to notice your pain. They didn't abandon you physically, but emotionally. You already felt disconnected from your father when he started drinking, and now if Mom and Dad are fighting, you were left wondering "who's going to love me now?"

Even though we can't change what happened, God, unlike all the king's horses and all the king's men in the nursery rhyme, can recover your shattered, young, and tender psyche. There's no explaining this other than to say that he, being God and our Creator, is able to put us back together. No matter what happened to us along the pathway of life, he can restore the shattered pieces of your soul. The power of God has just given you an object lesson of Psalm 23:3, "He restores my soul."

CYNTHIA: You really know how to make things clear.

COACH: Let's thank God for what just happened. "Lord, we thank you for your healing, powerful presence. Thank you for exposing the bruised place in Cynthia. Thank you for your wisdom, understanding, illumination, and power. Thank you for your never ceasing love for us. I acknowledge your grace working actively in Cynthia's life. I pray that she will continue to grow in her relationship with you. Amen."

CYNTHIA: Amen. I feel so much better. Thank you so much. Oh no, what time is it? I have to get home, change, and get to work. I have to go. I'll see you next week. Oh, what's my homework for this week? Let's not forget the homework.

COACH: Actually, you'll have two for this week. The first has two sections, and the focus is learning how to be still in God's presence. It contains a word of prophecy that the Lord gave to me several years ago. The second one will help you discover your anxious places. In doing your exercises make sure you are in a quiet place. As you do your assignments guard yourself from interruptions, and don't rush through them. Take your time.

*As soon as I handed her the exercises she made a mad dash for the door. That girl is always in a hurry.*

*Even though Cynthia hurried out the door, she drove home at a snail's pace. She felt so calm that she didn't want to disturb her profound sense of inner peace.*

Now that was something else. Oh my god! I can't ignore the fact that something happened deep inside of me. I never realized how much that situation scared me. Coach was right, that really messed me up. I know I'm not making this up, but I actually feel stronger and more stable inside. It's just hard to explain. I don't even know who I can tell this to. This is one of those times that I wish I could call Eric.

# Chapter 10

Over the span of two years Cynthia had accumulated over a month of personal and sick days, so she took the day off. It seemed perfectly rationale to use some personal days since God was personally working on her. She dedicated the whole day for doing both of her assignments from coach.

After taking a long walk in the neighborhood, Cynthia returned to her condo, showered, dressed, and ate lunch. When she made up her mind to do something, she did it. She was now ready to do the assignments. Her life was always full of interruptions, and she didn't want any during her day of introspection. She ignored the flashing message light on her telephone, turned off her cell phone that had both voice and text messages that needed responses. She already knew there were at least 120 e-mail messages to answer, so she didn't bother turning the computer on. She grabbed a box of tissue, her journal, pen, and a bottle of water. Knowing that she would be there awhile, she positioned herself comfortably on the couch, determined to complete both assignments before the day was over.

"Be still and know" was the first assignment. Be still? Now that's a concept most "New Yorkers" have yet to embrace. The constant hustle and bustle is what made New York so exciting for a Cali girl. It took some time to get used to the busy pace of Manhattan, but a few months she began to thrive on the synergy. Having a type A personality, it was difficult for her to be still. After weeks of hectic going, going and still going day after day, Cynthia slowly relaxed. She was surprised to feel all the tension in her body and vowed to be still again real soon on a massage table. Cynthia prayed and read the assignment.

## Be Still and Know

# Part I
### Position yourself in a peaceful still, quiet place.

**Be still and know that I Am God . . . (Ps. 46:10)**

Blessed are those who dwell in your house: they will be still praising thee. Selah. (Ps. 84:4)

Be still people, we are too *busy,* slow down! God wants us to learn how to be still. According to Psalm 23:2, the Lord leads us beside still waters. Everyone knows the calming effect of a lake or ocean. God has provided in nature places that are designed to woo us to relax and commune with him. God desires to impart peace deep within our souls that are more often than not filled with fear, worry, anxiety, and stress, all of which disrupts our ability to relax. Relaxation is vital for soul restoration. Being still puts us in a frame of mind that is conducive for reflection and meditation on the one who is higher than I. This is the place where you come to know with confidence that he is God, and you are not. In stillness we are positioned to hear his still, small voice ready to guide, impart wisdom, comfort, or revelation. We are his workmanship, and as we submit our soul issues and concerns to his care, he will give us peace. And as we do, God is busy at work transforming you from the inside out, replenishing the tired, bruised, shattered, and wounded soul with healing grace and living water. As you behold him, you will be changed by him, in divine increments, from glory to glory to glory. It's amazing what a rested, well-nurtured, spirit-refreshed soul can endure, create, and accomplish.

§

# Be Still and Know
## Part II
**Position yourself in a peaceful still, quiet place**
**Read the following out—loud and very slowly.**

I am more than just a higher power. Why have a spirit guide when you can have me, the Almighty God—up close and personal. I am calling and drawing you closer to me.

I am not too big or too busy for you.
I am not a distant Ruler reigning in some distant heaven.
I am *not* so preoccupied with the big issues of the world that I don't care about you

I never have and never will forget or abandon you.
Nor am I angry with you.
You may be mad at me for allowing certain things to happen in your life.
All I can say for now is that I will overshadow the pain you have experienced.
I know how to turn ashes to beauty if you would just trust me.

You may never fully understand some of the situations that occurred in your life, but I do.
I ask that you learn to trust me. I know it may be difficult for you to do that, but I am wooing you back to me—gently, gingerly, and most assuredly.

I want to be intimately connected to you so that I can nurture you with a love like none you've ever known—safe and gentle, patient and forgiving.

I have a plan for your life, and as my plan unfolds, you will realize that you have great purpose and significant contributions to make while you are on this earth.
I want to encourage, affirm, and empower you. I am grooming you for your unique greatness, and guiding you in the direction of your destiny for my glory.

I'm so glad you're inviting me to be more intimate with you. I will teach you how to recognize my voice and receive my love.
I will teach you about yourself.
Only I know you completely. You have seen only glimpses of who I created you to be.

When I lead you to difficult places, those that have caused you deep pain, be confident in me. I will release my power to heal, reconstruct, and realign you. I am preparing you on purpose for your purpose, My purpose.
As you abide in me, I will reveal truths to you that will set you free. Remember that I love you utterly, completely, and unconditionally. I just need you to . . .

*Be Still and Know That I am God.*

§

"OMG, I can see why being still is necessary for the soul. It's the time when you get to enjoy the simple things of life, smell a few roses and spend quality time with God. Brenda always talked about having a relationship with God verses being religious . . . Oh I get it now. I always thought God had a time quota I had to achieve before I could get his ear. Boy, was I wrong? He wants me to acknowledge him and be with him. OMG."

Cynthia couldn't write fast enough. So many wonderful insights were pouring into her and she needed to get them out in writing. She didn't want to miss any insight, revelation, or direction the Holy Spirit was freely giving to her. After a full hour of mediating and writing in her journal, Cynthia took a break.

Cynthia was so relaxed that she actually took a nap in the middle of the day. Taking a nap at any time was unheard of in Cynthia's fast-paced life. After three hours, Cynthia woke up and was surprised that she had slept that long. Apparently, she was tired. Her body knew it, but her take charge demeanor would not accommodate her body's request for rest. She felt so much better and realized that life's simple pleasures, like taking a nap in the middle of the day, doesn't cost a dime. Perhaps this revelation would help her to stay on her budget.

Cynthia woke up feeling rested, refreshed, and was ready for the next assignment.

§

### Discovering Your Anxious Places
### Psalm 139:23-24
**Pray, Read, Meditate, Pray, Read, Meditate . . .**

"Hum, I don't think I like the title. It sounds a bit scary. As a matter of fact, I'm anxious already. Actually, anxiousness is a feeling that I have had for most of my life. I just never knew how to describe it, or what to call it. I thought it was a normal state of being since we live in such a busy world and drink too much caffeine. I was shocked when the coach helped me to understand anxiousness is not a feeling that you should have as a constant companion. Lord, thank you for coach." Cynthia was so grateful.

After slowly reading the scripture several times, Cynthia took a deep breath, exhaled and prayed. "Lord, I give you permission to search my heart. Help me discover the anxious places in me. I realize now that these places have led me down the wrong path, many times in my life. I'm scared to see those places, but I trust you to lead me, comfort me, and once again restore my soul in Jesus' name, Amen."

Slowly thoughts of her childhood began emerging. Cynthia had a lot of great memories playing with her brothers and cousins. To her mother's surprise, Cynthia even got the little sister she always wanted. A smile emerged as she thought about how her mother had resisted the very thought of another child. Cynthia went into a closet and prayed that God would give her a sister and he did. Having faith as a child was easy, but then life set in and so did skepticism.

Her childhood memories, so distant, were like a forgotten dream. And though her childhood was filled with fun and laughter, there were also difficult times. Things that happened that she hadn't thought about in years and didn't want to remember. With those thoughts, she could feel anxiety creeping up inside her stomach. Although she realized that God was answering her prayer, it was a scary place for her.

The Holy Spirit brought back memories of Cynthia being depressed most of time as a child. The feelings of emptiness were at times overwhelming to the point where she didn't even feel real to herself. As far back as she could remember, she never wanted to be alone. If anyone tried to leave her, Cynthia would cry hysterically. It was a good thing her father left for work before she woke up. She adored her father and couldn't wait for him to come home from work. When his truck pulled up, she and her brother would run to the door and jump on top of his shoes. They would take turns as their father would swing them through the air with the greatest of ease. Every night, Cynthia's would lay on her father's lap as he sang to her and rubbed her back. She would fall asleep feeling loved, peaceful, and protected. Then one day without warning, the bonding time came to an abrupt stop. Her home slowly became a scary place where Daddy's mood could change in a second without any apparent cause. What happened? Her father started coming home late and wouldn't get a chance to see his daughter. And during the rare times that she did see him, he was always mad about something. Slowly but surely her dad turned into someone Cynthia no longer recognized. "Who was this stranger? Why is he yelling, cursing, and . . . hitting my mom? Who is this man and what has he done with my daddy? Oh no, no I don't want to feel all of this." Not wanting the panic to take her over the edge, Cynthia reached for her phone. As if on autopilot she called Eric. She sighed and thanked God when he didn't answer. Finally, Cynthia was able to calm down and began to think about her spontaneous reaction to the anxiety she was feeling. Cynthia came to a powerful realization; whenever she felt vulnerable, she would automatically and desperately reach for a man. She also made the connection that her innate response stemmed from feeling disconnected from her father's love.

Thoughts of her childhood once again began to resurface. She started remembering all her friends in the neighborhood. They had so much fun growing up in a Calder sack. She especially had fond memories of one neighbor in particular, Marc. He was Cynthia's very first boyfriend. Even though it was considered puppy love, since they were only six years old, Cynthia and Marc had a very strong emotional bond. One day, on the playground at school, some boy started to hassle her. All she had to do was to call his name, and Marc would swiftly come to her rescue. She pictured herself like the lovely damsel in distress she watched in her favorite cartoons. She had her very own handsome prince. Marc was her hero, and she needed him, but she was only six years old. Could it be that her need for Marc's love replaced her father's sudden lack of attention? Yes, another piece of the puzzle came into focus.

At six years old, Cynthia longed for true love, the stuff that fairy tales are made of. She took on the persona of a princess who needed to be rescued. Like Sleeping Beauty, Cinderella, Sweet Polly Pure Bred, and all the other fairy tales and cartoons she watched on television and read in books, she expected a knight riding a white horse to show up one day. She was always in anticipation of her Prince Charming. The one who cared enough to find, rescue, and love her. She wanted her very own happily ever after ending.

From Marc to James, from James to Michael, from Michael to Donald, From Donald to Charles, from Charles to Martin, . . . she couldn't recall all of the names. During her junior year in college, she did something she had vowed never to do. She had a relationship with a woman. At that time her best friend became "the one" available to love her right then and right now. Cynthia always felt she could not survive without being in a relationship.

I wonder now, "How I could have been oblivious to the fact that I was in one committed relationship after another from the time I was six years old." It was back then that I learned how to flirt. Now, as an adult, I had perfected the art. It was a power I had. Like a spider, I could pull anyone into my web. It mattered not whether they really cared for me. Now that I think about it, I may not have really even cared for them. I pretty much accepted anyone that came along. All they had to do was pay just a little attention to me. Hum, maybe that's why I married my first husband. I didn't really love him, but I married him anyway. I then understood that the thing that mattered to me the most was that *somebody, anybody* was there.

Once I had a boyfriend, I would do everything in my power to keep him.

I remembered the songs I sung as a teenager when I was in a relationship. I became Chaka Khan, Diana Ross, Jennifer Holiday, Pattie Labelle, Brenda Russell, or whoever else was singing passionate love songs on the radio. I would sing the lyrics to the top of my lungs. *If you leave me now you'll take away the biggest part of me . . . ou ou we e no baby please don't go . . . Through the Fire to the limit to the wall for the chance to be with you I'll gladly give it all . . . Ain't no mountain high enough to keep me from getting to you . . .* Singing those songs were my love anthems and vows to my current boyfriend. Oh god, you're showing me all the illusions I was creating subconsciously in my mind as I sang those songs. I was constantly giving love and never received enough to replenish what I gave out. At least I had someone in my life, even though I got little in return. I went from one relationship to another. I compromised my standards. "Did I ever really have any standards?"

Thoughts of that traumatic night, when I saw my parents fighting surfaced again. But this time, I didn't feel the deep hurt or sadness. Hum, Jesus can heal emotions and memories. As I thought more about how I took charge of the situation, I saw myself as a little scared girl who all of a sudden transformed into a fearless heroine and handled it. I realized that I always took charge and handled the frantic urgent need I had to find someone to love. "Why am I *so* needy? . . . Why do I have to be loved *so* badly? . . . and why was I always rushing from one relationship to another?" She could clearly see how her childhood perception of losing her daddy's love impacted and affected all of her relationships. She cried at this realization, but this time her tears felt like a release of internal pressure rather than grief.

And then the phone rang. "Oh, hi, Eric. *She had forgotten to turn the phone off when she called him earlier.* Yes, I did call earlier, but I didn't leave a message. Yes, it has been a long time since we've been together. A nice dinner tonight would be perfect. Okay, where should I meet you? Sounds good, I'll see you at seven."

He wants to take me out to dinner. Do I really want to do this? Well, at least I won't have to cook, and I won't have to clean up the kitchen. Sounds like a plan to me. What shall I wear? Um . . . something . . . tight and sexy. I want him to see what he's been missing.

# Chapter 11

When she arrived at the restaurant, Eric was already there. Kissing her on the cheek, he handed her a single red rose and a blue Tiffany bag. He always showered her with beautifully wrapped gifts, and Eric always enjoyed watching her open them. Cynthia was delighted that the content of the bag was a bracelet she showed him on their last shopping trip. She hugged him, and he held her tightly. He wouldn't let her go, and Cynthia didn't want him to. She found herself thinking about the more pleasant times of the relationship. At times he could be so thoughtful, and this was certainly one of those times.

They ate, talked, laughed, and reminisced over the good times; they were once again enjoying each other's company. Eric apologized for throwing her Bible across the room and explained why he did it. His mother was very religious and always tried to shove the Bible down his throat. It wasn't that he didn't believe in God, he just didn't like the way his mother tried to force him to be religious. After being together for nearly five years, that was the first time he ever said anything to Cynthia about his relationship with his mother. His extreme reaction now made sense, and she had no problem forgiving him.

Cynthia could tell that Eric had a session with the coach. He wasn't arrogant or sarcastic, and he revealed things that he had never spoke of before. As he shared his childhood with her, they both felt closer than they had ever been. Reminiscent of their early dates, they talked as the restaurant staff cleaned up for closing. After noticing their evil looks, Eric placed a large tip in the waiter's hand and thanked him for not kicking them out. Eric was the classiest man Cynthia had ever dated.

Not wanting the night to end, Cynthia asked Eric to come over for a nightcap. One thing led to another, and against her better judgment, they made love for the first time in a long time. Eric fell asleep, holding Cynthia in his arms. Cynthia laid there quietly crying, and these weren't happy tears. Lying in his arms had always been a comforting place for her, but this time she felt empty.

After a rather sleepless night, Cynthia felt awful the next day. She tried to identify the emotions but couldn't; they were just so convoluted. She put on one of her best designer suits in hopes that it would make her feel better, but it didn't. Putting on her best clothes and shoes always made her feel better, so she knew something was definitely wrong. She called the coach for an emergency session. She couldn't wait a whole week, and thankfully coach had an early evening cancellation. Cynthia felt a little better, knowing she would soon be able to talk this all out.

When she came downstairs, Eric was in the kitchen cooking breakfast. She thanked him for the bracelet but made it clear that she was not ready to resume the relationship just yet. And then she told him that what she really wanted was him, not trinkets, no matter how beautiful. She braced herself waiting for Eric to get defensive, say something smart or blow up. She was shocked when he kissed her on the cheek and told her to have a great day.

§

Eric just couldn't get it out of his head Cynthia called her Tiffany bracelet a trinket. "Hum, I spent a lot of money on that so-called trinket." I must be losing my grip. I know how to give her things . . . gifts beautifully wrapped with something sparkling inside. Or something with a name like Prada, Gucci, or Dior. I love watching her open those gifts. Her eyes light up, and that million-dollar smile . . . I love that smile. Even if she was mad at me, I could change all that with just the right present. I thought the Tiffany bracelet would work like a charm, but now, she wants me. I always used gifts to pursue her, and even though I thought she was worth chasing, I was never sure what I would do once I caught her.

I don't live or want the playboy life anymore, but I don't know how to be a husband. I guess you could say I'm stuck somewhere in the middle. If I was to marry anyone, it would be Cynthia, but honestly the thought of being married scares the hell out of me. What's marriage all about, anyway? My parents never got married and my father left one day with I was 3 years old. I don't know anything about being married. I don't even know if I'm the marrying type. I'm not sure if I have what it takes to meet all of her needs, financially yes but emotionally no. It feels like I'm just going to be sucked into a black hole of her needing me too much. I don't want to marry her and then disappoint her if I can't live up to the marriage vows.

On top of all of that, now she's starting to read the Bible. She never did that before. Although she really doesn't talk to me about the Bible, in the back of my mind I wonder if she is expecting me to go to church with her. I'm not trying to do all that Christian stuff. I'm glad she accepted my apology for throwing her Bible. I sure hope God forgives me for disrespecting his Book.

Okay, enough already, all this thinking is stressing me out. Let me think about something else, something more productive, like how I am going to get that promotion on my job. Now that's what I should be thinking about. I get the results from my job performance review on Thursday. I generated so much money for the company this year, and at the end of the day increased revenue is all that matters. I have certainly paid my dues, and this time the regional big shot better get it straight. This is the third time I have been overlooked for the position. It's like I'm invisible or something. If it happens again this year, I'll really make myself invisible and quit. I'm sick of this bull . . .

Eric continued to vent for three hours.

# Chapter 12

COACH: Come on in, Cynthia. You look tired.

CYNTHIA: I am. I didn't get much sleep last night. I had so much on my mind, hence the emergency session. I'm so glad you had a cancellation and are able to see me.

COACH: Well, since this is an emergency, let's get started. Tell me. What's on your mind?

CYNTHIA: Well, I completed my first assignment—Be still and know. I was on the top of the world. God really spoke to me through that. I had time with God like I've never had before. Me? I thought that was only reserved for the real holy people. Not somebody like me. It was just like when I'm here with you. Wonderful! So many things are different about me. I almost don't recognize myself anymore.

COACH: You're turning into a new creature.

CYNTHIA: What?

COACH: Let's just say, old things are passing away. And now you see new things on the horizon.

CYNTHIA: I just love the way you explain things. I can really see what you mean. But . . . when I tried to do the second assignment—the anxious places, I just could not get through it. A lot of things were beginning to make sense, but I just couldn't continue. This kind of work is way too exhausting.

COACH: Yes, I agree it is hard work, but you're doing great. I'll walk through the exercise with you. Keep in mind this is a process, old things are surfacing so they can pass away. Always remember, you get healed as you go. Keep going, don't get stuck or paralyzed in the pain. God doesn't want your painful past to block your abundantly blessed future. Keep going.

CYNTHIA: My father used to always tell me how determined I was. He liked the fact that I never gave up. So I already have it in me to keep going. I assure you. I'm not giving up on myself. If I did that I would also, in a way, be giving up on God. With all that I have learned and experienced about God I just can't do it. He's becoming too real to me.

COACH: I see you brought your journal?

CYNTHIA: Yes, I remembered so many things about my childhood. Things I hadn't thought about in years. So I wrote them down along with some insight. First of all, I loved my parents, but I have to be truthful, my father was an alcoholic. Whenever he would be late coming home from work, I would get scared. When I heard him enter the house, I would instantly wake up. I would listen for a while to see if there was going to be any trouble. If all seemed well I would eventually fall back to sleep. I did this for years. I believe this is why I'm a light sleeper. And then somehow, I don't really remember how, but I found out that Daddy kept a gun in the house. I always had thoughts of him shooting all of us. I was an emotional wreck from that point on. I never knew what was going to happen.

COACH: Living in a home environment of substance abuse, or any abuse for that matter, has damaging psychological effects on children. I'm beginning to think that post-traumatic stress syndrome isn't just a condition for soldiers coming home from war. It seems yellow crime tape around the home has taken the place of a white picket fence. Truly, we live in a fallen world. Please keep talking. What else do you remember?

CYNTHIA: I thought about my first boyfriend. We grew up on the same street. It was sweet and innocent enough, but it really was more than just puppy love. We had a real emotional commitment. Then, it dawned on me. What was I doing in a relationship like that at the age of six? And then from six on, I was in a series of committed relationships. I was always looking for someone to love me.

COACH: Age six, that's the age when you saw your parents fighting, right? Remember in our last session when you said "who's going to love me now?" That thought, "Who's going to love me now" was a mantra coming from a childhood anxious place. This hidden theme fueled your continual search for love.

CYNTHIA: Oh . . . okay, I can see it now.

COACH: As you were making these significant connections, how were you doing emotionally?

CYNTHIA: Not too good. I felt that pit of emptiness again. I just stopped and put the homework down. I actually felt numb. Even though I understand all the connections that led me down the wrong paths in my search for love, I don't know what to do about it.

COACH: That's okay. This is not a hurry-up-and-get-over-it process. I want you to acknowledge the fact that you now notice your emotions. The old you would suppress your emotions, the new you is working through them. It's a process, and you are progressing. Let that be your focus. Go ahead. Tell me what did you do in the thick of the emptiness?

CYNTHIA: I called Eric. I automatically picked up the phone and called him as soon as I felt that emptiness come over me. It was like I was on automatic pilot or something. He didn't answer. I didn't leave a message, but he did eventually call back. He wanted to take me out for dinner. I thought there was no harm in having dinner with him, but I asked him to come home with me and . . . I slept with him. I was so mad at myself. I cried all night.

COACH: I see, and now you're feeling guilty.

CYNTHIA: Yeah, and I'm so mad at myself.

COACH: Cynthia, you were going through an emotional rough patch and you wanted to be comforted. Based on the history and origin of your romantic experiences, being in a relationship was always comforting for you. But as you continue to build your relationship with God, you will come to know his heart and thoughts toward you. And you will learn how to let him comfort you. He, the Shepherd, wants to lead you in the way everlasting . . . his ways . . . his paths. God loves you, Cynthia, even when you make wrong decisions. He's not going to leave or abandon you on this journey. He's going to lead and counsel you. He is in the process of perfecting you, bringing you into maturity. Be confident that he will give you insight, understanding, power, and strength along the way.

The Lord is revealing the roots of your anxious thoughts and at the same time constructing something new in you, a root system that is attached and anchored in him. It may feel a little unstable at first but eventually, as you stay connected with God, you will become stable in his love. It's like when you transplant a plant to a bigger pot. The roots have to get accustomed to the new soil. As you stay connected to him, your roots go deeper in the rich soil of his love. With time those anxious places will no longer lead you down the wrong path.

CYNTHIA: I get it, but it's so hard for me to know that kind of love. I know Jesus died on the Cross for the sins of the world. But I could never grasp the fact that he loved me. Are you sure he still loves me even when I mess up?

COACH: Oh, please, we all mess up. We have all missed the mark in our relationship with God, but he's made provisions for our shortcomings. He looks beyond our faults and sees what we need. He sees the original place of abandonment from both of your parents. You can clearly see how your father abandoned you emotionally, and I'm very sure that your mom was struggling with depression herself. She probably wasn't able to handle your emotional needs too well. All of our parents missed it in some way or another. It doesn't mean that they didn't love you. It just meant that they needed some emotional healing of their own. I want to share another scripture with you. It's found in Psalm 27:10 (NKJV). "When my mother and my father forsake me then the Lord will take care of me." Your mom and dad did in a way forsake you, but not intentionally. As they were fighting, they didn't notice your pain, and certainly could not console or comfort you. The Lord is taking care of you. I assure you he is aquatinted with your grief. Let's pray and see what else the Lord wants to do.

Father, Cynthia and I come to you. We thank you for your abiding love that remains with her even when she struggles. I thank you for the power of the blood of Jesus that heals and cleanses her. I thank you that your love is being shed in Cynthia's heart. Thank you, Holy Spirit, for revealing the embedded psychological triggers that lead her down hurtful paths. Thank you for your Word that encourages, gives hope, wisdom, and direction. Your strength is being perfected in her weakness and for that, we give you praise. She is your child, and your love is now raising her up in those places where others dropped the ball. With your supernatural power, you are healing her from damaged emotions, replacing the internal garment of fear and anxiousness that she has worn for most of her life. You are doing exceedingly abundantly, more than she could ever ask or imagine by your power that is working in her. Thank you for loving her beyond her personal faults and seeing what she really needs. Let your presence continue to bring light to her path. Continue to manifest your consistent love for her and to her. Let your peace and grace be multiplied in the name of Jesus. Amen.

*Once again the power of the Lord was present to heal, and Cynthia was captured in his presence. She could no longer sit up. She laid her head on the couch pillows and closed her eyes.*

COACH: How are you doing?

*I asked reluctantly. I didn't want to interrupt what the Lord was doing.*

CYNTHIA: I'm good . . . Thanks for praying . . . I . . .

COACH: Don't try to talk right now. I don't what you to disconnect from God's presence too quickly.

*Cynthia's face had a soft, radiant glow. This kind of beauty has nothing to do with makeup. Under the shadow of his presence, Cynthia received just what we needed from, the loving presence of God.*

CYNTHIA: Oh my . . . I never knew prayer could be so empowering. As you were praying, I literally felt the guilt lifting off me and strength coming into me. It's like each word you spoke produced a surge of hope and peace deep down inside of me.

You know, this process is very difficult but very rewarding at the same time. I'm gaining so much. I know that God is leading me to a better life. I'm becoming inwardly stronger, more stable and secure. It's just so hard to explain. I am so thankful for our time together. God bless you, Coach.

COACH: Thank you, Cynthia, God bless you too. See you next week.

CYNTHIA: Do I have a homework assignment?

COACH: Just one, go do something fun for yourself this week. Believe it or not, that's your assignment. You're too hard on yourself.

CYNTHIA: Oh, no problem, I know I can do that. I just have to do it without maxing out my credit cards.

Cynthia walked out of the session without her companions, guilt, and shame. The power of God's love had lifted the burden and empowered her with strength. She began to sing a song she learned in Sunday school. "Love lifted me, Love lifted me. When nothing else could help, love lifted me." She sang it over and over again. Who's going to love me now was no longer a hidden impetus. That question was settled to the core of her being, "God loves me, and he's going to love me both now and forever more. Lord, thank you for lifting me up where I belong." Any song she could think of concerning the love of God, she sang to the top of her lungs. With the same deep, passionate intensity she had when singing about her past relationships, Cynthia sang to God. She was in a new relationship, one that would be a love affair for life.

# Chapter 13

On Thursday morning, Eric arrived early for his appointment with the regional director Mr. Randle. He wore a new navy blue suit in order to look like the part of a high class executive. He learned long time ago that it was important to dress for success. "Fake it till you make it" was his rational for buying most of the suits in his closet. He was confident that his performance review would convince the corporate heads to finally give him the promotion he desired. Anticipating the adulation of his coworkers, Eric practiced his acceptance remarks. Not wanting to appear too prideful, he planned to keep his speech short and simple. He even made reservations at Cynthia's favorite restaurant to celebrate. Even though he knew that she wanted to take a break from him, he also knew that she would never refuse a celebratory lobster dinner.

Eric: Good morning, Mr. Randle.

Mr. Randle: Good morning, Eric. Come on in. Would you like a cup of coffee before we go over your evaluation?

Eric: No thanks, I've already made my Starbucks run.

Mr. Randle: All right. First let me start by saying that you have done an excellent job this year. The partners and I are impressed with all your hard work. Your production over the past year has increased and the numbers are quite impressive.

Eric: I guess all my strategies paid off, especially with that six figure deal. It was a piece of cake.

Mr. Randle: Yes, it was very lucrative indeed. All of our clients speak very highly of your work ethic and actually prefer working with you over anyone else.

Eric: Well, that's good to know. Complete client satisfaction has always been my top priority.

Mr. Randle: Yes, all of your scores in that category are stellar. You also have high marks in staying on target with both the budget and finishing each project on time.

Eric: I worked very hard to improve in those areas since my performance review last year. I know that a VP must always deliver the goods on time as promised.

Mr. Randle: Why yes, of course, timeliness is an attribute anyone in upper management must have. However, before you get ahead of yourself, I must share a concern that I have. In speaking with your team they have complained that you have been, should I say, not as professional when dealing with them. Most of them have said that you are sarcastic, arrogant, and seem mad most of the time. Quite frankly, they say you are very hard to work with. As you know, it is imperative for a VP to foster a positive working environment to keep the team motivated. Because of this, Eric, the partners and I feel that you are not quite ready to become a VP at this time. Actually, from everything I've heard, it is our recommendation that you attend the next anger management workshop offered by our training consultant. The human resource department will inform you when the next one is scheduled.

Eric was livid and fought hard to keep a poker face. He concluded that his coworkers were jealous and intimidated by his potential. Sabotaging his promotion made something clear, they all had the crabs in the barrel mentality. Of course they would pull him down before he made it to the top of the heap. But the straw that broke the camel's back was the suggestion of taking anger management classes. Eric decided that he'd better quickly get out of that office. If he had waited just a few more minutes, his actions would prove them right.

ERIC: Well, if that is it, Mr. Randle, I'd like to get back to my office. I don't agree with my coworkers comments, but it's your decision.

Eric was able to maintain his cool demeanor as he shook hands with Mr. Randle. He also kept a straight face as he walked swiftly past the cubicles where the "backstabbers" were working. Another motto that Eric lived by was "never let them see you sweat," and he didn't. He promised himself that he would quit if he was overlooked again, but he quickly reneged on that one. He had too many expenses. He wished he hadn't bought the brand-new suit he was wearing. He could have easily worn something else. An hour before the workday ended, Eric left the building. He had a session with the coach and needed some time to get his game face back on.

Eric's secretary was anxiously waiting for his arrival. If he got the promotion, she would also be promoted. Eric always told Robbie that she was the best administrative assistant he ever had. He promised to take her with him when he made it to the top. Robbie had already earmarked her upcoming bonus for a down payment for a new car. She visited a new car lot and had already picked out her brand-new Lexus. Robbie was so sure that Eric would get the promotion; she talked with the sales assistant and assured him she would be back to get her car. When Eric walked through the door, without saying a word, Robbie knew that her beautiful new car would remain on the dealership lot. Eric headed straight to his office without speaking, and Robbie gave him his space. She had worked for him for years and knew this wasn't a good time to have a conversation with him.

A wave of anger overtook him. With one forceful sweep with his arm, everything on his desk hit the floor. Robbie rushed to the door and peeped in. "Are you all right? Can I get you anything?"

Seeing the mess he had made, she offered to clean it up. "Yes, I would appreciate that. I'll make it worth your while." Whenever he said that, Robbie knew a sizable bonus was right around the corner. Eric may have been a lot of things but stingy wasn't one of them. "No problem, I'll be happy to do it."

"Great, I'm going to take the rest of the day off. Don't call me unless somebody is dead."

Eric went home, took off his new suit, and poured himself a stiff drink. After pouring and drinking several martinis, he took a nap.

# Chapter 14

Eric arrived at my office on time today. As a matter of fact, he was actually ten minutes early. Hmm . . . I guess traffic wasn't all that bad today. As Eric walked in, I could tell he was upset about something. Throwing his coat on my couch was a dead giveaway that something was up.

COACH: Good afternoon, Eric. How are you today?

ERIC: I'm okay. I just had a hard day at work.

COACH: Is it something you want to talk about?

ERIC: No, not really. It's no big deal.

COACH: All right then, let's get started. Is it okay with you if I start by praying first?

ERIC: Sure, go ahead. I'm sure it won't hurt. Besides, I probably need some prayer anyway.

COACH: We all need prayer, Eric. Father, in the name of Jesus lead us in this session. We want to discover your plan for Eric during this time. I praise you now for what you are going to show us. Thank you for your grace, mercy, and favor resting upon him now, in this moment. Amen.

ERIC: Amen.

COACH: What would you like to discuss today?

ERIC: Well, Cynthia and I hit another wall, but I'm sure she told you about that in her session. I have some things I want to say about that, but before I do, I think I need to get something off my chest.

COACH: That's fine. Is it about your job?

ERIC: Yes, it is. I had my yearly performance review today with the regional director of the company. I have been trying to get a VP promotion for the past three years, and once again it didn't happen. I am so tired of trying to get the position that I know I deserve! I had promised myself that if I didn't get it this time, I would just hit the door and never look back. I quickly came to my senses as I thought about my credit card balances. I owe American Express, Visa, and MasterCard too much money to quit my job. I'm just stuck, I guess.

COACH: I'm sure that's very difficult for you after three years. Tell me why you believe you deserve the promotion?

ERIC: I'm the best producer in the whole company. I've made the most money for the business so far this year, and when it comes to getting contracts, "I'm the man." Everybody knows that. I don't get it. I should have been VP by now.

*As he talked, I could hear the frustration rising in his voice. Although he was trying hard to control his anger, the tone of his voice and his body language gave it away. I suspect that his anger goes much deeper than the job situation, but I knew he wasn't quite ready to hear that from me just yet.*

COACH: Did your supervisor give you any reasons why you were not promoted?

ERIC: He mentioned some things my team had to say about me. My coworkers must have filled his head with lies in order to stop me from getting to the top of the ladder.

COACH: What exactly did he say?

ERIC: He said that my coworkers complained that I was arrogant and sarcastic, and that I was hard to work with. I really don't care what they think. I can do all of their work with my eyes closed. They are just a bunch of jealous idiots. And then he had the audacity to say that I needed to go to some anger management class. That's just a crock. He's probably intimidated by me and thinks that one day I'll get his job.

COACH: Eric, can I be honest with you?

ERIC: Sure. Isn't that what I'm paying you for?

COACH: I really do understand your supervisor's concern. You have a sarcastic edge that comes out periodically. And although you are self-confident, sometimes it does come across as being arrogant. I actually think you could benefit from anger management classes. After all, it couldn't hurt.

*I could tell that he wasn't happy with my comments. I set there waiting for a few snide remarks.*

ERIC: Oh, you think so?

COACH: Yes, I do. It's obvious from some of the things you just said and the way you said them. My guess is that there's a lot of anger under those remarks.

ERIC: I'm sure you would be angry too if you were overlooked time and time again. And for the record, I'm really not that sarcastic.

COACH: Yes, I probably would be upset. However, I would also try to figure out if there was any truth to what was said. Eric, why are you so angry?

ERIC: I thought I already answered that. I'm mad because I'm the best man for the job, and I don't get the respect that I deserve. I'm sick of the patronizing pat on the back for a job well done. It's like they don't even see me, like I'm invisible or something.

COACH: You mentioned that you felt invisible, tell me more about that. Is there any other time when you felt that way?

ERIC: I used to feel that way about Cynthia. I always tried so hard to please her, but she never acknowledged the good stuff that I did. She was constantly complaining about what I didn't do. That always used to set me off. But since coming to you, she's changed. She doesn't nag me about every little thing. She's not clingy, and I don't feel swallowed up by her emotions. I do like the changes I see in her.

COACH: Is there anyone else besides Cynthia who treated you like you were invisible?

ERIC: I'm sure you already know the answer to that question.

COACH: No, I don't. That's why I asked.

ERIC: Okay . . . all right already, my mom. She pretty much ignored me since I was sixteen.

COACH: Let's spend some time talking about that.

ERIC: Oh, you're really good. Here we go with the childhood stuff. Fine. What do you want to know?

COACH: Just start by telling me about your mother.

ERIC: My mother is a religious fanatic. After my father left us, she got a new man, and his name was Jesus. That's all she ever talked about. Jesus this, Jesus that. She was always talking about God, the devil, or the pastor. She quoted scriptures to me like a drill sergeant. She would say things like, "As for me and my house we will serve the Lord." Okay, that meant me. I was the only one in her household.

Every time I made her mad, she would say, "Eric, God don't like ugly." She tried to make me conform to all the rules and regulations of Christianity. As a teenager, I went to a party where some of the guys had gotten a hold of some liquor. I tried to take a sip, but all I could hear in my head was the eleventh commandment, the one my mother added to the original ten . . . "Alcohol is *never* to touch your lips!" And . . . oh, there was always the holiness or hell line I heard often over the pulpit, and my mom made sure that it was repeated in the home. "I know, Mom. God don't like this, God don't like that . . . I know, I know."

I grew up in the church. I was always at church. I had no choice. We were there every time the door opened, and always one of the last to leave. On Monday nights, we went to Bible study, Tuesday night was prayer meeting, Wednesday was the midweek service, Thursday night was youth choir rehearsal, Friday night was witness training, and on some Saturdays, we had youth activities. On Sunday's, we were at church all day long. And please don't let it be the month long pastor's appreciation service, which resulted in an additional three o'clock service. And the sermons, I could never really understand them. Even in Sunday school, where they allowed us kids to ask questions, I never talked, I just mostly sat there and waited for the snacks. I had stopped asking questions a long time ago. When I realized that I could not ask a question without getting a full religious discourse that bored me to death, I stopped asking. And since I could never relate to what they were talking about, I stopped listening.

COACH: Can you remember anything positive you got out of going to church?

ERIC: Well, yes, I accepted Jesus as my Savior. As a teenager, I was in the youth choir, and I did enjoy being with the other kids there, but I saw and participated in things that should not have been going on in the choir room. Instead of trying to be a saint, I knew I was a sinner. I found it hard to keep all the rules and live holy. In my opinion, I was one of the biggest sinners in the church. So really, to be honest, since I couldn't live up to God's standards, out of reverence for the Lord, I stopped going to church. From then on, my mother went to church by herself. She was so disappointed in me. She has pretty much ignored me since then. She left me home by myself and continued to go to all her various church meetings and functions. I got into a lot of trouble when I was alone. I started selling drugs and was sent to juvenile hall for a while. Those "scare them straight tactics" they used worked on me. I made sure to stay out of trouble when I got out.

*As Eric continued, I heard something different in his voice. He didn't sound angry, he sounded disappointed. He was sad about disappointing his mother and God. He's still carrying a load of guilt.*

COACH: Well, I can certainly understand your frustration. There are a lot of things that we need to address. However, since we're short on time, we will have to continue next week. I have an assignment for you to complete before your next session.

ERIC: I knew it was coming . . . the *assignment!*

COACH: Yes, how did you ever know? Also, remember to say a prayer before you start working on it. Now let's close out our time with prayer.

*During his first session, Eric bowed his head in defiance, but this time, he did so with respect. The Holy Spirit was already softening his heart.*

Father, I thank you that you know Eric completely. You know his heart and you understand the source of his anger and frustration. Cover him with your grace as he does this assignment. I ask that you would replace his religious upbringing with your divine fellowship. Show him that you are for him and not against him. I ask that you would bring peace to his spirit regarding the job situation. Bless him with your guidance in Jesus' name. Amen.

ERIC: Amen. That's the first time someone has prayed for me, and I didn't feel guilty afterward. Thanks. I'll see you next week, and I'll be on time from now on.

COACH: All right. That's good. See you next week.

# Chapter 15

When Eric got up the next morning, he contemplated whether or not he should go to work; he found himself talking out loud.

"Since they didn't have enough sense to promote me, than who? God, I sure hope it's not Robert. He's has wanted that position ever since he joined the team two years ago. That just goes to show how naive he is. You can't get a position like that unless you're done the time. Two years are not going to cut it. He has a long way to go before he pays all his dues. Beside all of that, he's nowhere as good as me. If I have to answer to him, I'll probably just lose it. At least, I'll know for sure that I need some anger management classes. If that fool turns out to be my boss, I'll be first in line to sign up for that stupid anger management class. They should choose Lawrence. He's really the next best choice after me. Yeah, he's the most logical choice. He's really a smart guy, and we get along pretty good. If it can't be me, I bet it's him. Well, since we don't find out until tomorrow, I think I will take the day off. I don't want to be around those backstabbing cutthroats. Yeah, I'd better go ahead and take the day off, so I won't hurt anybody. They can just call on my cell if they need too." It was time for what he called the triple threat combo pact for relieving stress and tension—a good workout, the hot sauna, and a deep tissue massage. Eric headed for the gym.

After six hours of his relaxation ritual, Eric returned home with a clear head and tension-free body. He dreaded the thought of turning on his cell phone. Sure enough, he had seven messages from the office, all from Robert. "I may be hard to work with, but I'm still the one they call for all the answers. Robert, better not be the new VP." Eric refused to let the office drama sabotage his day of relaxation. He planned to work on his assignment in peace. "Whatever they want, it can wait. I'll deal with whatever it is tomorrow. I hope they don't ruin the company before then. Today, office drama is not allowed, I have an assignment to do." After making a fresh cup of coffee, he sat down and began.

§

How deep is your love for God?
Pray before answering the questions.
Keep the prayer short, simple, and to the point.

How deep is my love for God? That's easy to answer, not deep at all. And now I'm supposed to pray after, just confessing that I don't have much love for him. Man, what am I going to say to God? I'm sure he doesn't want to hear anything from me. I sure hope he doesn't strike me down while I'm talking. But on the other hand, if he wanted to strike me down, he would have done it by now. God is merciful; I know that for a fact. So I'll start with what I already know about him.

"Lord, you are so merciful, and I thank you for that. Your goodness and mercy really has followed me all the days of my life. I know you haven't heard from me in a while. No, you haven't heard from me in a very long time. I'll try to do better. Now, Lord, you know I don't make promises I can't keep. So even though I'm talking to you, I'm not ready to go to church or anything like that. I feel bad about asking you for anything knowing I haven't lived my life for you. But for now, I'm just asking that you give me insight as I complete this assignment. I hope this prayer meets with your approval. Amen."

### Question 1
### Do you love God?

Do I love God? Well, to be honest, I can't say that I do. Cynthia always says that if I love her, I should show it. According to her, actions speak louder than words. Those shiny trinket gifts were my actions, but anyway . . . so if that premise is correct, I guess I don't love God. Since I don't go to church or read the Bible or pray, I guess that proves it I don't love God very much at all. When I left the church and my religious upbringing, I put God out of my mind. I probably love him on some level. I remember saying the sinner's prayer as a boy. I came to the altar one Sunday when the preacher invited us to pray for salvation. He had just finished one of those fire and brimstone messages and told us that by receiving Jesus into our heart that we would not go to hell when we died.

When he gave the altar call, I was the first one out of my seat. I did not want to go to hell!

I was baptized that same night and given a brand-new Bible. I was to bring it to church every Sunday. I also remember being confused about what I was supposed to do next. Does this mean I can't go to the movies, to dances or parties, and what about bowling? I wasn't sure what being saved was all about, but I was glad I wasn't going to hell.

I got involved in all the church stuff. I sang in the choir, went to all the services, and participated in the special day programs. I faithfully said my Easter speeches, and I even went to the denominational state conventions. I did all the Christian things, but I can't say that I ever thought about God while I was supposedly serving him. After leaving the church, the next time I thought even about God was when I was locked up in juvenile hall for selling drugs. I hated that place. It was so hard for me to pray. I always felt like a hypocrite when I did. I didn't feel worthy enough to have my prayers even considered. I didn't think it was right for me to talk to God just because I was in trouble. I wasn't going back to church when I got out, and I didn't want to make any promises to God I couldn't keep.

I also thought a lot about my father while I was there. He was a career criminal. He spent more of his life in prison than out. When I was a boy I wanted to be just like him, but when I got out of juvi, I wanted nothing to do with him or that kind of lifestyle. When I got out, I stopped hanging out with the wrong crowd and started to excel again in school. I graduated from high school with a high GPA, and my SAT scores were also notable. So much so, that I was offered a full scholarship to New York University. My mother was so proud that I had finally got it together, but she was also afraid for me to go to college. She didn't want me to be enticed by all the sinful pleasures lurking in the dormitories. I have to admit it, she was right. I was always hanging out in the dorm, smoking weed, partying, and doing other things I don't want to ever think about again, ever. During those parties, way too much was going one. The morning after one of those "girls and boys gone wild" festivities, my friends and I were walking to class, and we saw the strangest thing. Right there in the quad, this dude with a Bible in one hand and a megaphone to his mouth was preaching. My friends were laughing at him and began teasing him. I was the only one not laughing; I couldn't join in with their jesting. Deep down inside, I wanted to stop them and say, "Are you guys crazy? Don't do that. Don't mock God!" But I didn't say anything, I felt like a coward. I should have said something, but I didn't want to get religious all of a sudden after being stoned with them the night before.

I called my mom and told her about the incident. I confessed to her that I knew I wasn't living right. I even asked her to pray for me, and of course she did, right then on the phone. I cried as she prayed, but as soon as I hung up the phone I went straight to my dorm room, rolled a joint, and got high. Although I appreciated the prayer, I felt guilty because I knew I wasn't going to turn my life over to God.

I did have one friend in college who was a Christian. Even though Michael was a strong believer, he didn't seem religious at all. He was so down to earth with his Christianity. He knew my sins, but never judged me. He once told me that even though God didn't like what I was doing, God would never stop loving me. He talked to me about his relationship with God all the time, and I always listened. Unlike my mom, Michael was never pushy, judgmental, or condemning with his faith. I was impressed with his relationship with God. It was like he and God had some kind of special connection. One day, I told him that the devil was too strong for me to deal with. And then he said something that just blew me away. He told me that the devil didn't have any power over me. I was literally stunned by that statement. I remember that conversation like it was yesterday. That Sunday, I went to church with him, and I really did get something out of the sermon. It was like the pastor was speaking directly to me. But when alter call was given, I cringed. Something in me wanted to run to the altar like I did as a child. But I made myself stick like glue to my seat. I had vowed a long time ago that I would never join another church.

Michael and I lost connection after graduation. But I will never forget the impact he had on me. Wow! I haven't thought about him in so long. I wonder what he's up to these days. Well, on to the next question.

## Question 2
## Do you believe God loves for you?

Nope. How could he? I haven't done my part. I wasn't trying to live for him, and to be honest, I still don't want to. How could he love me? He's probably sitting up there in heaven looking down on me and shaking his head saying, "Boy, you're always blowing it. When will you get it together?" He's probably sick of me by now. I always have the thought that one day he's going to just drop the ax on me when he's had enough. No, God couldn't love me. At best, he probably just tolerates me.

I do remember learning the story of the prodigal son I heard when I was in Sunday school. This guy took his inheritance and made a mess out of his life. But when he came back to his father, he was received with open arms. But there is a difference between me and the prodigal son. He wanted to go back, but I don't. So once again I ask, why in the world would God still love me? I guess in some ways he does. Like most people, I have been blessed. But come on, doesn't his patience run out sooner or later. I've heard it said that God loves unconditionally, but it seems to me love always comes with some kind of conditions.

I'm supposed to close out the assignment with prayer: "Lord, here I am. If you are still in my life at all, I ask that you just have mercy on me a little while longer. One day, I'll get it together where you're concerned. That's all I can say for now. Amen."

# Chapter 16

On Thursday morning, everyone on the sales team arrived to the office on time. Mr. Randle called us into the conference room to inform us of who got the promotion. "First, I would like to acknowledge the great work your team as accomplished. It's been a good year so far. Thank you all for a job well done."

After interviewing so many qualified candidates for the position, the executive management team and I had a difficult time making our decision. That just goes to show you how many great people are on your team. However, after much deliberation, the management team unanimously agreed . . . Congratulations to Robert Stevens!

Everyone began clapping, and Eric just about lost it. Robert walked up wearing a brand-new navy blue suit. Eric was fuming. Robert shook hands with Mr. Randle and was given a coffee mug, a pen set, and a briefcase that was worth at least $300. Robert was beaming with pride as he graciously received each gift. With a proud look on his face, Robert began his acceptance speech. After the meeting, everyone except Eric walked up to congratulate their new VP.

Eric decided that the best thing for him to do would be to quickly return to his office before he cussed anyone out. Slamming his office door, Eric paced back and forth talking to the air. "I knew it . . . they picked Robert over me? That's just crazy. I can't even take a day off without him calling all day long. Robert absolutely has no skills to handle the nuts and bolts of this organization." Eric continued to gripe until his secretary informed him that he had a phone call. It was his mother. "Great, what does she want now?" I swear, if she starts whining about anything . . . *Hey, Mom, what's up. Oh yeah, I forgot about the concert . . . it's this Saturday? Sure, I'll go with you, no problem. See you on Saturday. Bye.*

My mom . . . she's always been a piece of work. When I was growing up, not only did she put the religious guilt trip on me, she always smothered me with her constant hugs. As far back as I can remember, she would often cry and complain about my dad while she held me like some kind of teddy bear. I always felt like I was my mother's emotional babysitter. She was emotionally fragile and always depended on me for support. She even once told me that I was the only man in her life, besides Jesus. That statement always pissed me off. I didn't want to be all that to her. I wasn't a man. I was just a kid who wanted to ride my bike and play with my friends.

My parents were never married. They lived together until I was three years old. But till this day, my mother is still in love with him. I was the bargaining chip she used to manipulate my dad to spend time with her. One time, when I was in middle school, my mother devised a scheme that she thought would be fool proof. Knowing that my parent–teacher conference was coming up, she called my father two weeks ahead of time to talk to him about the conference, and how I needed help. According to her, I was getting low grades. She lied; I had all B's and one B+. I wondered how she would cover the fib during the actual parent meeting. She finally convinced him to meet us at the meeting, or so she thought. Well, of course my dad was a no show, and she cried all the way home. We never discussed my progress at school. Once again, she used me as the lure to draw my dad to her. It was never about me, but always about her. My job was to console her . . . "Don't cry, Mom, maybe he'll come to the next one."

Let me stop reminiscing; I have a lot to do. My new supervisor Robert, now how can I say that with no sarcasm, just sent an e-mail requesting financial projections. He wants the report on his desk before I leave today. Ugh! I don't know if I can do this.

# Chapter 17

It had been three weeks since her last session, and Cynthia was feeling great. She was enjoying her life and finally felt fulfilled. This was the feeling she expected to have once she was married. She had wasted years of her life unhappy because there wasn't a man in her life, and now to find out that she could have been happy all along was mind-boggling. The old Cynthia would have deep regret for every year wasted, and then internally attack herself for months. The new Cynthia rejoiced, praised, and thanked the Lord for healing her shattered soul. And even though she knew becoming whole would be a lifelong process, the results were definitely worth it. She thought about what the old people used to say in the church, "I'm not what I should be, but I thank God I'm not what I used to be."

She was also once again enjoying her relationship with Eric. After working one week with Robert as his boss, Eric came to some realizations concerning his relationship with Cynthia. She was always there for him; Eric often called her his personal cheerleader. And whenever he was frustrated, hearing her voice had a calming effect on him that he could no longer deny. It seemed that his life worked a lot better when Cynthia was in it. Eric wanted to respect her wishes for space from the relationship, but he took a chance and called. He began the conversation coming straight out with his true feelings for her. He loved her and said it. He wasn't hiding behind fancy wrapped expensive gifts; he was giving Cynthia what she wanted and needed, his heart. Cynthia of course was delighted to finally hear Eric say the words that any girl wants to hear from her man. But she was more overjoyed by the fact she was doing well before he started calling again.

§

When it came to her job, Cynthia was a perfectionist. Thankfully those who worked with her had thick skin and understood her quirks when it came to meeting deadlines on time. Cynthia came to work on Monday refreshed from a great weekend with Eric and was ready for a productive workweek. She sat at her desk and was alarmed to find an urgent memo on her desk informing her to go straight to the boss's office as soon as she arrived. Cynthia could not figure out what this was about. Frantically she turned to her planner and there it was. She forgot to schedule the deadline for a report her boss had requested. As Cynthia walked down the hallway, she felt like a little girl who was in trouble. It brought back memories of being summoned to the principal's office for being tardy for her first period class. She thought of all the excuses she could use as to why the report was late. Although she knew she could muster up a seemingly valid reason, she chose to take full responsibly for her actions. As she expected, her boss was fuming. Cynthia admitted her mistake and promised to turn in the report by the end of the day.

Returning to her office, Cynthia reverted back to her pre-sessions with coach days. The new Cynthia was kind and gentle to herself, but in this instance, the old Cynthia resurfaced. Her thoughts about herself were critical and relentless; she was her own worst enemy. Even though Cynthia was very intelligent, deep down in the core of her being, she was very insecure. Based on her external appearance and personality, no one would ever suspect that Cynthia had low self-esteem. She needed to be perfect at all times. If she failed to do or be so, she would discount all the wonderful things about herself. Eric complained about her constant nagging comments toward him. He had no idea she nagged herself even more.

After about ten minutes of self-annihilation, she finally took note of her thoughts. She was appalled at how she was thinking and finally understood why Eric refused to listen to her constructive criticisms. What she thought was constructive was actually destructive. She could feel the impact of her negative thoughts. Depression slowly, covered her like a blanket. But instead of allowing herself to be wrapped tightly in clutches of her own self-criticism, she made a choice to counteract the power of her negative self-talk. She thought about her sessions with coach, the homework assignments and the simple prayers. Cynthia took a deep breath, calmed down, and became still before God. She recalled the scriptures she had studied and prayed out loud in the privacy of her office.

"Lord, I thank you that even when I make a mistake or encounter situations that are out of my control, you never condemn or criticize me. Please help me stop being critical of myself and others. I ask for the peace of your presence, I ask for wisdom as I write this report, and I trust that thou art with me. Thank you, Lord, for leading and guiding me in Jesus' name. Amen."

At the end of the day as promised, Cynthia placed the complete report on Ms. Goodlow's desk. The next morning, Cynthia had an envelope on her desk. It was from her boss. She felt anxious as she opened it, bracing herself she read the letter, "Cynthia, this is the most concise yet informative report you have ever submitted. It seems that you work very well under pressure. Thank you for being diligent to turn in the report as promised. I appreciate that." Ms. Goodlow.

# Chapter 18

It had been a month, and so far Eric had maintained a professional demeanor working with Robert, but he wasn't sure how long he could hide his true feelings. Eric did not respect his new boss and was still angry about not getting the position. It didn't help that Robert had already made several bad decisions, and Eric had several ideas to undermine his authority. Fortunately for Robert, Eric was not a vindictive person and would never carry out his backstabbing plans. But he did know that his frustration would be expressed with full force sooner or later.

On top of having to deal with Robert, Eric dreaded his decision to attend the church concert with his mother. At the thought of dealing with Robert and his mother in the same week, Eric called to see if it was possible to have a longer session with coach. He was willing to pay for the extra time.

§

COACH: Come on in, Eric, the receptionist informed me of your request for a longer session. I can do that, must be something serious going on.

ERIC: Yes, I have a couple of things I want to talk about. I'll start with my mother and then my so-called boss.

COACH: Okay, sounds like a plan. Let's pray: Father, we come acknowledging you always. You already know the things Eric is carrying in his heart. Help him to articulate what's in his heart. Supply us with your wisdom for this moment. Amen.

ERIC: I got a call from my mother reminding me that I promised to go to a concert at her church. Really I had forgotten all about that concert. I guess I just blocked it out of my mind.

COACH: Why would you feel the need to block it out? Does your mom still give the guilt and silent treatment tactics?

ERIC: No, she's much better now. She started going to a new church and since then, she's a lot better. I just want to be fully prepared just in case some manipulative residue happens to spring up from out of nowhere.

COACH: Got ya . . . and your boss?

ERIC: He's nowhere in my league. I'm not trying to be arrogant or anything, really I'm not. It's just the truth. Isn't there a scripture that says you shall know the truth and the truth shall set you free? I'm just being truthful. As a matter of fact, I'm brutally honest most of the time.

COACH: Okay . . . but there's also a scripture that says we are to speak the truth in love, not brutality. I think there is more truth for you to consider.

ERIC: What truth are you referring to?

COACH: The truth that your inability to work well with others caused you to lose out on the promotion you were qualified for.

ERIC: Touché, I guess you're right. I never looked at it that way.

COACH: Did you bring in your assignment?

ERIC: I have it right here.

COACH: Okay, how did you answer question 1?

ERIC: I told you about my mom always dragging me to church and how I got tired of going. But as I answered the first question: Do you love God? I remember a time when I did. I was about twelve years old when I prayed the sinner's prayer and asked Jesus to come into my heart. I was so happy that I wasn't going to hell, and in my own way, I was grateful to God for that. I wanted to please him, but over time I put God on the back burner of my life.

COACH: Was there anything in particular that caused you to put God in the back of your life?

ERIC: When I was three years old, my dad walked out of the house and out of my life. He never married my mom and didn't stick around long enough to be a father to me. I knew plenty of kids whose parents were divorced, but they spent time with their fathers on weekends, summer break, or for the holidays. I rarely saw my father. I would call and leave messages on his phone, asking him to take me to a game or show up for my school programs, and he would always promise he would, but he never did. After that he stopped returning my messages. I just couldn't understand why he was always missing in action. Even if he couldn't be with my mom, why couldn't he just be there for me?

In Sunday school, I learned that if you prayed, God would answer. I prayed the same prayer every night. "Now I lay me down to sleep, I pray to the Lord my soul to keep, if I should die before I wake, I pray to the Lord my soul to take . . . and please God make my dad come over and spend some time with me. Amen." The next morning, I would sit by the window and wait for my dad to walk up the driveway, but he never did. God never answered. And since my father never came home, I stopped going to God's house. Don't get me wrong. I still have respect for the Lord, but I stopped expecting him to answer my prayers.

COACH: I see. Is your father still alive?

ERIC: Yep, he's alive and well. He's been residing at the state penitentiary for the last sixteen years. Even though my mother would not allow me to go to the prison to see him, she insisted that I always buy him a Father's Day card. Do you know how hard it was for me to buy a Father's Day card for him? No card ever expressed my true sentiments. I remember staying in the store for over an hour reading each card and saying to myself, No, I can't say that. No, that's not what he did. No . . . Nope . . . Naw . . . They don't make cards that say, 'Hey, Dad, where are you? I wish you would show up more often.

COACH: Tell me about your father.

*Eric laughed softly to himself. Here goes the childhood stuff again. How did she manage to sneak that in? She's good.*

ERIC: On the rare occasions when he would show up, I was always glad to see him. He had a lot of style. He wore alligator shoes, sharp leather coats, and a Rolex. He drove a silver Jaguar and was without a doubt "Mr. Bling Bling." He was a real ladies man too. I guess I got that trait from him. Every time I saw him he was with a different woman, and I thought that was so cool. He could get any woman he wanted, like James Bond and Billy Dee Williams. My papa was definitely a rolling stone. He had a constant string of women in and out of his life. We never had much time alone, with all those women around, but I didn't care. I was just glad to be with him.

As I got older, the visits were less. When I was graduating from high school, I called my father and begged him to come to the ceremony. I was one of the keynote speakers for the event, and I wanted him to be there. I had turned my life around and went from a street thug to a valedictorian, with a full scholarship to NYU. I wanted him to be proud of me. As always, he promised to come, but as usual he didn't show up. As I gave my speech, I searched the audience looking for him. When I realized he wasn't there, I kept looking at the door, hoping he would walk in before I was finished. He never did. I found out later that day that he had been arrested the night before. The police had finally caught up with him. He's still in prison. He's been in and out of prison for most of my life. I think he's scheduled for release sometime next year.

COACH: How did you react when you found out that your dad was going to prison for so long?

ERIC: I just made a joke about it, but the joke was on me. Even though I was graduating with honors, I felt so stupid. I should have known he wouldn't show up.

COACH: I admire the fact that you're able to talk about all of this. How do you feel about what you just said?

Eric: After years of trying to be like my dad, I decided that I didn't want to be anything like him at all. As a matter of fact, I wanted to be the exact opposite of him. So I got myself together and went to college.

Coach: How do you *feel* about all that you just said?

*Eric replied in a joking manner.*

Eric: I don't have feelings.

Coach: Hmm . . .

*I didn't even respond to that answer. I just sat there relating to the little Eric trapped inside a grown man's body. In his previous session, Eric mentioned that he felt like he was invisible. I could really see why he felt that way. That little boy felt invisible to his mom, dad, and God. My thoughts of this smart unnoticed little boy made me silently pray for him. I asked God for wisdom. Lord, please give me the words that will speak your heart concerning Eric.*

Eric: Why the serious look?

Coach: I'm thinking about everything you said, just give me a minute . . . how did you answer the second question: Do you believe that God loves you?

Eric: I'm not even sure he likes me. I think he does. I don't know.

Coach: Well, first of all, I can assure you that God loves you. And secondly, I want you to know that as you were talking earlier, I paused to absorb and feel everything you said, how you said it, I heard your disappointment. You hardly saw your father, and your mother was always at church. It's no wonder you felt invisible. And I understand why you would feel invisible by your company. Consistently being rejected for that position triggered the "I am invisible to people switch."

*Eric wasn't arguing or joking. He was listening attentively to every word. God was breaking into his prison. This captive was on his way to being set free.*

ERIC: I don't know what to say. I can't even think of a joke or a sarcastic remark. For once I'm stumped.

COACH: You don't have to say anything, just listen. Your disappointment is valid. You felt rejected and abandoned by both parents. A young child does not know how to interpret rejection from a parent. A seven-year-old boy doesn't come up to his father and say, Father, I am very hurt and disappointed that you never keep your promises to me. A seven-year-old would slam doors, break stuff, or just be angry overall. If the anger is never dealt with, that same boy will grow up but will display the anger in some other form. I'll give you a perfect example that ingrained sarcastic edge of yours indicates unresolved anger.

ERIC: You're right . . . I'm angry at both of them. They were pitiful parents. I already know that the Bible says we are to forgive others. I can forgive my mom since she raised me all by herself. I can at least give her an "A" for effort, but forgiving my father, no way. I hope you're not going to ask me to forgive him. He doesn't desire my forgiveness.

COACH: Have you've seen a person who is handicapped in a wheelchair with their legs amputated.

ERIC: Yes, of course.

COACH: Well, I want you to consider this. Your mom and dad were also both crippled, you just couldn't see it. They were emotionally handicapped, and their emotional limitations have in a way handicapped you. In one way or another, we are all handicapped.

*Eric took my words to heart. His defensive demeanor was weakened, so I continued.*

Another important point is that if a child has misgivings concerning their parents, that child will have the same type of issues with God. For instance, since your father was absent from your life you probably feel that God is also absent. And since you were constantly disappointed by your father that disappointment will spillover into your relationship with God.

Eric: So, you're saying how I view my earthly father has influenced how I perceive God.

Coach: Exactly. You felt invisible to your mom, and you probably also feel invisible to God. Do you?

Eric: I can't deny that.

Coach: God does still love you, Eric, and you are not invisible to him. He's going to heal you. He's willing, are you?

Eric: I don't know. I don't think I can really make that kind of commitment to God.

Coach: Let me share with you why I believe you have a hard time making commitments.

I also understand why you would feel uncomfortable at the thought of marriage, which is also a commitment. I'll explain it to you, and you tell me if I'm right or wrong.

Eric: Since you're already on a roll, go for it.

Coach: All right. You never saw commitment from your father first of all. He always broke his promises to you. At one time your heart was open toward him, but he never kept his word. He was unable to keep a commitment. And on top of that, it seemed that your mom was more committed to the church than to you. You said in a previous session that you stopped going to church because you were unable to commit to all the religious rules and regulations, hence you respectfully backed away from God. I believe you really do want to get married, but that's also a vow, a commitment to both God and Cynthia. Your perception of being in a committed relationship means that you have to follow rules and regulations, and you don't want to take a chance disappointing either of them. Let me share another truth with you, God is still 100 percent committed to you. And yes, your behavior may not be the best from God's standpoint, but he's still committed to you. I have the perfect exercise that will help that truth sink into your soul.

ERIC: Okay, I can't argue with any of your observations. I look forward to this assignment, sounds like it's right up my alley.

COACH: All right, let's pray. Father God, thank you for revealing more truth to Eric. I pray that you would heal his heart from all childhood disappointments. I also ask that Eric would no longer see himself as a disappointment. Please help Eric forgive his father. His father didn't realize how his irresponsible behavior would damage his son. You are his father, Lord, show him how committed you are to him. Help him to see that you are a wonderful, Father. Remove all distorted perceptions that blocks your love from saturating his heart. Bring healing to his heart that he may be able to freely give and receive love. Show Eric how precious your thoughts are toward him. Thank you for perfecting everything that concerns him and confirm this prayer by your miraculous power in Jesus' name. Amen.

ERIC: Amen.

COACH: Here's your homework. I would like for you to write a reflection paper after completing the assignment. It doesn't have to be long. Take your time, meditate on the reading, and write from your heart. I know you will get a lot of insight from this one. I'll see you next week.

ERIC: Next week it is!

Eric walked out of the office, speechless. He had never heard anyone talk to him in such a reassuring manner. Finally, someone took the time to hear and really understand him. And from that moment on, Eric no longer felt invisible.

# Chapter 19

Coach was right; it took me about three days to really absorb this exercise. This one really made me think. The assignment was based on the Bible story found in Genesis 3; the fall of mankind. As a result of disobeying God's only request of them, Adam and Eve were put out of the garden of Eden. They were not to eat from the tree of the knowledge of good and evil. Why was that so hard to do? Well, I guess the devil made them do it. After all, Satan was the one who had deceived them. That snake worked overtime to make sure the first couple took in all of his lies.

My Bible had a vivid illustration that depicted the story. I still remember the drawing of Adam and Eve leaving the garden. Thunderbolts of lightening were hurling towards them as they were kicked out of their perfect abode. Wearing their self-made fig leaf garments, they left the Garden of Eden with their heads hung down in shame. God must have been really mad. He even posted a giant angel holding a huge silver sword at the entrance of the garden. His job was to block them from reentering the garden. With a stern, mean look on his face, the angel was serious about enforcing God's judgment. To me, that look said, "You'll never get back into God's good graces." It was the same look that I often got from the little old ladies at church when I was talking or playing during the preacher's long-winded sermon. Most of the time the ladies were nice, but they taught us kids that God doesn't play. With only a look, they could easily snap us into submission. I was actually afraid of God. I always saw him as the supreme chief of a supernatural cosmic police force. I guess that's why I always felt I had to duck and dodge him. I can't even imagine how Adam and Eve felt as they hid from God among the trees. They probably thought he was going to strike them dead.

As I continued reading, two things stood out that I had never seen before. It blew me away when I realized that Adam could still sense God's presence, and even heard God's voice after he disobeyed him (Gen. 3:8-10). But even more surprising than that, God was still talking to them. Unlike my mother when she was mad at me, God did not give man the silent treatment. Like a concerned father, God was calling out to man saying "where are you?"

Hum, I realize now, that God was trying to reach out to man. Even though they had sinned, God still wanted to have a relationship with them. I have to admit that as I continue to reflect on this, he's probably reaching out to me. He even exchanged their self-made fig leave garments with coats of skin that he especially made for them. A divinely crafted outfit, how's that for a fashion statement.

This assignment has certainly made me see God in a different light. Maybe my perception of God has been wrong all these years. Coach did explain that children often learn about God by watching their parents. If that's the case, it's no surprise that I would have a distorted view of his character. My mom always used God in a negative way to control me. I thought he was mad at me and ready to kick me out of his good graces. I can see how her misrepresentation of God made me misunderstand his intentions toward me.

When my prayer for my father to come home was never answered, I felt God was so unfair. I couldn't understand why I didn't have a dad to play catch, go fishing, or just watch football together. That would seem unfair for any child. Then it dawned on me, maybe God was actually protecting me by not allowing my father to come home. If my father had been in my life, I probably would have turned out just like him. And if that is the case, God did answer my prayer although his answer was no. I guess I'll just have to trust that Father God knows best, even in this situation.

I was always trying to earn God's love and never felt worthy to receive his help. I understand now that I, not God, condemned myself for every mistake I made. I wonder what would have happened if Adam and Eve had just admitted their sin and came clean before God. I'm sure things would have turned out much differently. Maybe that's exactly what I need to do.

It's really amazing how the Bible can speak directly to you. Those scriptures spoke to me loud and clear. I got it. Unlike my father, God never abandon me. Even when I felt that I had disappointed him, he was always there. I just didn't realize how much God still loves me.

*The powerful revelation of God's love poured deeply in Eric's spirit. He responded by actually getting on his knees and praying like he had never done before.*

Oh God, I'm sorry for running from you . . . for hiding and not trusting you. Lord, I got you all wrong. I can see your heart and your intentions toward me are good. I *have* heard you talking to me, but I just kept ignoring you because my focus was always on me and what I wanted. Please forgive me for being so stubborn and rebellious. I realize now that I broke up with you, and you never broke up with me. I'm sorry. I understand now that you want a relationship with me. I can see that clearly now. It's not about religion at all. It's about having a relationship with you. Thank you, Father God, for making provisions for me through the sacrifice of Jesus Christ so that I could be restored back into fellowship with you. I want to be in your presence. I come to you "naked"—truthful. I thank you for forgiving me for all the mistakes I have made. Lord, thank you for your patience and mercy toward me. Help me become the man that you created me to be. I ask all of this in Jesus' name. Amen.

After his prayer, Eric could literally feel the presence of God all over the room. He felt lighter as the peace of God flooded his soul. The only time he had felt that close to God was when he prayed to receive Jesus as a little boy. He now had realized what he had been missing, being in the presence of God.

He was in seventh heaven and wanted to stay in that place. He turned on the television and was surprised to find so many Gospel music channels. Turning to the Gospel oldie but goodies channel, a song that he used to sing when he was in the choir came on. "A Change a Wonderful Change Has Come Over Me . . ." Eric turned up the volume and started to sing. Unlike when he was young singing in the choir, Eric could now relate to the songs. When he was young, he sang without understanding the significance of the lyrics, but now those old songs actually made sense. For the next hour, Eric delighted himself in the Lord, singing and remembering all that the Lord had done for him over the years. He never knew that he could have such a good time with God without being at church.

# Chapter 20

Ever since Cynthia missed her project deadline, she felt she needed to redeem herself. Although her boss was pleased that she did get the report, Cynthia was still embarrassed that she had dropped the ball in the first place. Everyone in the office referred to her as a perfectionist, and she didn't want to ruin her reputation. She worked day and night the following week just to make sure she stayed on target with the financial statement that was to be included in the quarterly report. Vowing that she would never make a mistake like that again, Cynthia was determined to submit her report two days before the deadline. As she carefully checked her figures for the third time, she happened to glance at the clock and panicked. She was going to be late for her session with coach. The last time Cynthia was late, even though it was only by five minutes; she promised coach that she would never be late again. Once again Cynthia started to internally attack herself, but didn't. Instead she phoned coach to make sure it was all right for her to come twenty minutes late. She was thankful that coach was so flexible.

§

CYNTHIA: Coach, I'm sorry. I'm late. I was working and lost track of time.

COACH: Oh, that's okay, you're hardly ever late.

CYNTHIA: I know, but I hate being late.

COACH: Yes, I know you do. But, Cynthia, nobody's perfect. You really need to give yourself more grace.

CYNTHIA: I know. I'm learning. As a matter of fact that's exactly what I want to talk about in our session. Something happened at work last week that really upset me.

COACH: Okay, let's get started. I would like for you to say the prayer.

CYNTHIA: What, me . . . pray out loud? I never pray out loud.

COACH: Just keep it simple. You can do it.

*Cynthia hesitated for what seemed like a good three minutes. She took a deep breath and began.*

CYNTHIA: Lord, I want to thank you again for being with me. Please bless me with more insight and understanding. Reveal whatever you want to show me during this time. I thank you in advance for what you are about to do in this session. Amen.

COACH: That was perfect! Go ahead and tell me what happened at work.

CYNTHIA: When I came to work on Monday morning I had an urgent memo on my desk, I had missed a deadline and was summoned to my boss's office. Sure enough, I neglected to schedule the date in my organizer. I felt so stupid, that's something an intern might do, but me? As I scurried to her office, I literally felt like a little girl who was in trouble and was told to go to the principal's office. My boss was angry, and I had no recourse. I assured her that before the day was over I would have the report on her desk. When I got back to my office, I was so hard on myself, just like you mentioned. I could not believe that I had missed that deadline. I always aspire to do the best at being professional, missing a deadline that important was just inexcusable. I felt embarrassed, humiliated, and self-conscious. I thought about those who were affected by my mistake. Was I the hot topic at the water cooler? Was I being judged and criticized? Did they think less of me? I knew I would be at the center of the office gossip for at least a month. I could feel anxiety in my body, and was approaching the point of no return, depression was about to overtake me. Then I noticed my internal dialogue and realized that I was my own sternest critic. I was over exaggerating the whole situation. I was not incompetent, ineffective, or stupid, but I was saying all of those things in my mind. It was just one mistake and it could be rectified. It wasn't the end of the world or my career. I sat still for a moment, calmed down and prayed. I asked God for peace and was finally able to pull myself together. I worked all day and actually finished the project. By 2:00 p.m. I gave the report to Ms. Goodlow.

COACH: Oh, Cynthia, I cannot tell you how proud I am of you. You may feel that you still have a long way to go, but let me tell you what I see. First of all, you were in touch with how you felt at the moment. In the past, you would automatically suppress your feelings. Then you took note of your self-loathing thoughts, that's major. On top of all of that, you incorporated the be-still-and-know exercise, you got still and prayed!

CYNTHIA: I have been in touch of my feelings ever since you show me the "How do you feel" chart. I do see the progress, but I still have a long way to go before I conquer my tendency to self-destruct in my own mind.

COACH: You are going to surprise yourself, I assure you. One day, instead of automatically thinking negatively about yourself when you fall short of perfection, you will automatically nurture yourself with positive self-affirmations.

CYNTHIA: That's just so hard for me to believe.

COACH: Yes, but you've also made great progress, and it's very important to take note of the subtle transformations that occur along the way. Always remember that you get healed as you continue the journey to wholeness. God has begun a good work in you, and he will complete it. Being grateful for each step that is made in the right direction, honors what the Lord is accomplishing in you.

CYNTHIA: I am very grateful. Thanks for sharing that with me. I never want to diminish what the Lord has done for me.

COACH: All right. Let's talk more about some other things I heard you say. You mention that you felt like a little girl being called into the principal's office. I believe that is a significant realization, and our prayer focus for today will center on that statement.

Lord, thank you for bringing Cynthia this far, and we acknowledge the significant growth in her. Your Word assures us that you will complete the work you have begun and for that we are indeed grateful. And now, Father, I pray for the little girl Cynthia, who surfaced as she walked to her boss's office. Shine the light of your love in the deep dark places of her soul that holds the key to this realization in Jesus' name. Amen.

*When I pray for someone, I usually keep my eyes open in order to notice any reactions during the prayer. I could see by the look on her face that she was upset.*

COACH: What's going on, Cynthia, how are you doing?

*After a long pause, she finally answered.*

CYNTHIA: I feel frustrated and angry.

COACH: Why?

CYNTHIA: I don't know. I think God is showing me something, but I'm not sure.

COACH: Just start by telling me what you are sensing right now. You already said you were feeling frustration and anger. Do you know who you're angry with?

CYNTHIA: . . . I'm mad at . . . myself. Missing that deadline was so stupid . . . a lot of things were just out of my control. I did the best I could under the circumstances, but it just wasn't good enough.

COACH: Cynthia, what circumstances are you referring to? Are you referring to your job or is it something else.

CYNTHIA: At first I was thinking of the job situation, but all of a sudden my thoughts changed to my parents.

*Cynthia was apparently agitated, her voice was trembling and although she was on the brink of tears, she would not allow herself to cry.*

I can't believe I wasn't able to stop them from fighting, I tried so hard. I'm so mad at myself . . . I feel like I dropped the ball. I should have done more.

COACH: Cynthia, you were only six and that situation was completely out of your control. Even though you did the best you could, it was not your responsibility to fix your parents' marriage, stop your father from drinking, or become the savior of your family. You couldn't change what was going on in your house, it was out of your control.

*When working with small children, I usually give them paper and crayons and ask them to draw a picture of what they experienced. Since Cynthia was a child at the time when she was trying to stop her parents' fights, I thought the same technique would work for her. I gave Cynthia some blank pieces of paper and told her to draw what she believed the Holy Spirit was revealing to her. As she started to draw, I prayed silently.*

CYNTHIA: God showed me a little girl. It's me. I'm standing in the doorway of my parents' room, and I can't move. I'm looking at my six-year-old-self, frozen at my parents' doorway. I see her just standing there, and it's getting on my nerves.

COACH: You're angry with her, why?

*I could hear the anger and frustration in her voice as she began to speak.*

CYNTHIA: . . . Because she's just standing there doing nothing. She just can't stand there and do nothing. She needs to take charge of the situation. She needs to do something!

*By this time, Cynthia was actually yelling. I knew it was time for a divine exchange. I took her hand and explained what the Holy Spirit was revealing.*

COACH: When you entered your parents' room and saw what was happening, there was a part of you that froze in fear. But another part of you pushed past your fear and took charge of the situation. Now I'm not saying that you have multiple personalities or anything like that, but when you instinctively sprung into rescue mode and got the help for the family, you left someone behind. That frighten, frozen part of you is still standing at that doorway. Now as an adult you still scold your frozen self. Therein lays the root of your proclivity of self-mutilation.

CYNTHIA: Oh my god! Yes, yes, you are so right. I don't like that part of myself. I can't stand weakness in myself or others. I was angry at my mother for allowing that kind of abuse to reoccur. She should have picked up a lamp or something to defend herself, and because she didn't, I saw her as being weak. I thought I would be much stronger if I was in that predicament. No man would ever hit me and get away with it. He would see no sign of weakness in me, *never!*

COACH: Are you still angry with your mother?

CYNTHIA: No, as I became older I understood her dilemma and I forgave her. It was very different for women back then.

COACH: Well, if you can understand your mother's position and forgive her, you can do the same for the six-year-old you. Surely, you can also see and understand that a six-year-old-girl would be frightened to death by what you saw. You did great by getting help during the crisis. You felt that it was your responsibility to take charge, and you handled it like an adult. You really were a responsible little girl. However, it's time to go back and get the six-year-old you abandoned. It's time to forgive her. It's time for her to be rescued.

CYNTHIA: Oh, I get it. I did abandoned myself. But how do I rescue her? I don't know how to get to that part of myself.

COACH: You can't, but God can. First, you have to forgive her, just like you forgave your mother for the weakness you saw in her.

CYNTHIA: I can forgive myself, now that I have a different perspective. Actually you helped me to reframe the situation. A six-year-old should not be frozen with fear, you're right. I have a niece who is six, and I can't imagine her trying to do what I did. I would never hold it against her, if she couldn't control something as major as that. I do forgive myself.

COACH: Wonderful, you can see how this incident left you in fragile pieces, but remember that God is . . .

CYNTHIA: Restoring my soul.

COACH: Yes, he is. Now I'd like for you to pray for your own emotional healing.

CYNTHIA: I'd rather you pray. I'm not used to praying in front of people.

COACH: You did a great job praying earlier. Besides, I want you to get accustomed to praying healing for yourself. That way you can have your own sessions whenever the need arises. Give it a shot.

CYNTHIA: All right. I see your point.

*Cynthia hesitated as if she was gathering her thoughts and searching for the right words. I hope she's not trying to pray a perfect prayer.*

COACH: Just keep it simple, Cynthia. You can do it. Go ahead.

CYNTHIA: Lord, I thank you for being with me. I pray for myself. I pray for the part of me that is frustrated and angry that I can't control everything. I pray for the part of me that is fearful and weak. I forgive myself, and I know you're healing me from the residue of the trauma I experienced as a child. I invite you into that pain in Jesus' name. Amen.

*As soon as she said amen, God quickly showed up, the spirit of the Lord was present to heal once again.*

COACH: What are you sensing, Cynthia?

CYNTHIA: I can see myself standing in the doorway. Inside the room I see my mother and father on the floor fighting, and in that instant, it's like I jumped out of myself and took charge. This is so weird . . . I can see the part of myself that was left behind. I look like a little puppy left out in the cold, so sad, scared, and lonely. I don't know what to do for her, and I still feel disgusted with her. My adult self wants to scold her . . . beat her up for being so afraid, but I know that is not the best thing to do. I really don't know what to do. There seems to be a gulf between us. She doesn't want to come to me, and I don't want to reach out to her.

COACH: Lord, we welcome your presence in this situation. Cynthia is stuck as a child and as an adult. Show the power of glory once again.

*By this time Cynthia had laid down on a pillow, she was so relaxed. Actually, she was in the best position to receive deeply from the Holy Spirit.*

CYNTHIA: Wow! I see someone coming to bridge the gap between the two parts of myself. I know it's Jesus. I see compassion and tenderness in his eyes. As he looks at me, I can feel strength emanating from him and that strength is being imparted into me . . . the frustration I felt with myself is dissipating, and I'm beginning to feel calm and peaceful.

He wants the adult me to embrace the abandoned little me, but I just can't do it. I realize that even the adult me is frozen . . . Jesus is showing me what to do. He has one arm wrapped around the little me, and he's motioning for the adult me to come closer. He placed his other arm around the adult me. Now he's embracing both sides of me. We are in a group hug—the little me, the adult me, and Jesus. That embrace feels so good, and I feel so secure. I don't see Jesus anymore . . . and now I'm embracing myself. The adult me and the little me . . . we're still hugging each other, and it's like we are meeting for the first time.

COACH: Stay in that place as long as you can.

*Cynthia was bonding with a lost part of herself. She started weeping, but this time her tears were ones of resolve, rather than an expression of pain or grief. Joy was rising up inside of her and a beautiful smile emerged. She lifted up her hands, began to worship the Lord, and wasn't concerned at all about her makeup or anything else for that matter. It was absolutely glorious!*

CYNTHIA: I feel so much peace. I don't understand it. I feel so secure. It's like his embrace brought stability to the anxious little girl part of myself and grace to my adult perfectionist self. I have never felt so peaceful. I can't explain it.

COACH: You're feeling the peace that surpasses understanding, shalom. It is difficult to comprehend, but it's very real.

CYNTHIA: Nobody's going to believe this when I tell them, I can hardly believe it myself.

COACH: That's because it's supernatural. Most people, even Christians, forget the supernatural workings of God. If he can part the Red Sea, he can certainly heal our emotions. You lost a piece of yourself and the Lord recovered it. He's always on a search and recovery mission on behalf of his children.

CYNTHIA: I never thought about it like that. I always believed a knight in shining armor would one day rescue me. I had no idea it would be God.

COACH: I am elated at what God has done for you. In each of our sessions, he has done so much for you. Eric is also doing well in his sessions. I meet with him next week. If all goes well as I expect it will, I'd like to see you both together after his session.

CYNTHIA: You know, Eric is going to a concert with his mother tomorrow. That should be interesting.

COACH: Yes, I know. I'm certainly going to keep him in my prayers. I'm sure God is going to do something wonderful with Eric and his mother. Let's believe for a good report.

CYNTHIA: Sounds like a plan. After this session, I definitely have faith to believe that it will be all good. Having a relationship with God makes all the difference in the world.

COACH: Yes, it certainly does.

# Chapter 21

After her sessions with the coach, Cynthia could barely contain herself. She had to tell somebody, but not just anybody. She had to tell someone who would really get it, someone who knew her inside and out, and of course that person was Eric. Besides that she missed him. Not the gifts or the sex, she missed him, the person. About a month ago, Cynthia was having problems with her car. She felt it was the perfect opportunity to call Eric. Of course, Eric came right over to help her out. He had the car fixed and paid for the repairs. Ever since that day, they slowly began to reconnect. With mutually agreed upon boundaries, they got back together. They reestablished phone calls, once a week daytime dates, no sleepovers, and no sex. Their intimate connection was no longer just a sexual one; it had evolved into a deeper, spiritual bonding. Their relationship was no longer based solely on their physical bodies coming together, their souls were uniting. The two were becoming one. They were enjoying each other again, laughing again, and were excited to be together again.

Neither one of them could contain themselves after time with coach. The sessions were always an amazing experience, and there was no one else they could really talk to about them except each other. They shared their individual sessions with coach, talked about the assignments, and marveled at the transformation they saw in each other. One beautiful Sunday morning while at breakfast, Eric and Cynthia did something that they had never done before. They prayed together. They both agreed that God had been the missing link in their relationship. Together, they made the decision to start going to church. As it turns out, the church that Eric's mom was a member of, was the same church that Cynthia had visited with her friend Brenda two years ago. Eric was going there for a concert with his mother on Saturday and decided to see if this was a good church for he and

Cynthia to attend. Eric laughed as thought about how his mother would respond if he surprised her by coming to church on his own. "Baby, I just had a vision of Mom literally passing out as soon as she sees us walking through the church doors. I hope they still use smelling salts like they did back in the day." They both laughed and walked out, holding hands. Their relationship was becoming stronger, and they gave all the credit to the Lord.

# Chapter 22

Eric drove slower than normal to his mother's house. Although he did visit his mother on occasion, he never stayed more than an hour. Tonight mother and son would be together for a lot longer than an hour. Eric didn't know what was in store for him, but he was determined to keep a positive attitude. When he finally pulled up to the house, his mother Diane was already at the curb. She had invited him to come to her new church several times but Eric would always come up with the perfect excuse to get out of going. He parked and got out to open the car door for her. She was so excited to see him; she hug and kissed him over and over again. "Son, I'm so glad to see you. I can't wait for you to see my new church. I have learned so much from the pastor's teaching. You know, he's not that much older than you. I bet you both have a lot in common."

"Well, Mom, this was the perfect time for me to come. You know how much I love concerts, and my work scheduled hasn't been too hectic lately." Little did Diane know, Eric was just excited as she. After spending quality time with the Lord himself, he was on another page spiritually. He just hoped his mother would not try to put any guilt trips on him for not coming to her church sooner.

Diane walked into the New Visions Christian Fellowship with her son, beaming with pride. She introduced Eric to several of her friends; Diane was elated. Eric was pleased to have put a smile on his mother's face. Before now, he could only picture that disappointed look she had for months when he refused to go back to church. This would be the first time that Eric stepped inside a church since he was sixteen years old.

The concert was excellent! The band was comprised of professional musicians, and the choir was outstanding. They had praise dancers and a banner ministry that really set the place on fire with God's presence. The focus was certainly not entertaining or generating hype. These people were true worshipers. There was a type of energy in the atmosphere that Eric couldn't explain. It was similar to what he felt when coach prayed, but a hundred times stronger; the minister explained it as the anointing. Eric had grown up in the church but had never known or experienced the anointing. If he had, he probably would have never stopped going. A lot had changed in the church world. Eric was pleasantly surprised by the sermon; the message was very inspiring, practical, and relevant. Eric was so impressed, and he was already planning to come back during a regular Sunday service and bring Cynthia with him. He knew she would love this church. Eric decided against sharing this information with his mother. He wasn't about to give her an open invitation to aggravate him with constant reminders of his promise to come back to the church. He knew that the surprise element was the best way to go.

After the concert was over, everyone was invited to the fellowship hall for refreshments. Eric got a chance to meet the pastor, and they had a great conversation. His mother was right, they really hit it off. He had never met a pastor who was so down to earth. Most preachers to him were so spiritual that they were no earthly good, Pastor Edwards was nothing like the pastors he had encountered. Diane continued to introduce him to everyone; she was ecstatic. He had always wondered why his mother didn't have any joy in her life prior to now. She always went to church depressed and would come back the same way. Why go church if after hearing a Word from God you still remained depressed. He just didn't understand that. But now he could see how happy his mother was, and that made him happy. "Son, would you mind getting me a cup of punch?" Diane could have gotten the punch herself, but her real motive for asking was so that more people could notice her handsome son.

"Of course, Mom, that's an easy request." Eric replied as he walked over to the table beautifully arrayed with flowers, cake, and cups of punch. As he got closer, he noticed a man who looked very familiar to him. Eric turned to get a better look at his face and got the surprise of his life. Standing right there next to the punch bowl was Michael, his old college buddy. They hadn't seen each other since graduation, eleven years ago. He looked the same as he did in college, only with a few more pounds and minus the gray strands of hair.

Eric walked up and tapped Michael's shoulder. Michael turned and was shocked. "Eric, is that you? I can't believe it." Michael was shocked to see Eric in the first place. But for them to reunite in a church setting was a miracle as far as Michael was concerned. He knew how much Eric hated going to church. Michael hugged Eric and laughed. "Of all the places for us to reconnect, in church, the time you went to church with me you flew out of there as soon as the service was over. What's up? Did hell freeze over or what?"

Eric chuckled, "Yea, I did hightail it out of there pretty fast, didn't I? All I can tell you is a whole lot has happened since then. We definitely have to catch up, but for now, let's just say that none of your prayers for me were in vain. I thought you lived in Miami. Do you live here now?" Eric hoped that was the case.

"Yes, I do. My company moved me here last month. So tell me, Eric, how is it that you're here, all up in the church house?"

Eric answered glancing around the room and pointed to his mother, "I'm here with my mother. She had invited me to the concert, and here I am."

"Really. My wife and I just joined this church last Sunday . . ." Before Michael could give more details, a very beautiful and very pregnant woman walked up and handed him a piece of cake. "Eric, this is my wife Denise. We're expecting our first child next month, it's a boy. Honey, this is Eric, my college friend I told you about."

Eric extended his hand. "It's nice to meet you. I hope he didn't tell you only the bad stuff."

Denise smiled and replied, "No, actually it was all good. It's great to finally meet you. You'll have to come over for dinner very soon." Eric gladly accepted the invitation and was looking forward to introducing Michael to Cynthia, and he already knew that Cynthia and Denise would become great friends.

"Michael, I hate to disturb your wonderful reunion, but I'm really tired, is it okay if we go home now?" Eric noticed the tenderness in her eyes and in her voice as Denise spoke to her husband.

"Eric, I hope you don't mind."

"Not at all, Denise. Michael, take this lovely lady home. We will get together real soon."

"Oh, okay, baby, no problem." Eric and Michael exchanged numbers.

"Perhaps we can catch a basketball game. Play-offs are coming up. You know that we never missed the play-offs back in the day."

Michael agreed, "Boy, those were the days. See you soon." Eric watched as Michael carefully escorted his waddling wife to the exit door. For the first time, Eric thought about what it would be like if he and Cynthia had a baby together. They had never had that discussion, but after seeing how happy Michael was, Eric thought it was time for he and Cynthia to talk about the possibility of having children one day.

When he told his mother about seeing Michael, Diane was happy to hear that news. She figured that since Eric already had a friend at the church, he would be more likely to accept her invitation to come back during a regular Sunday service.

During the drive home, Eric and his mother talked, laughed, and enjoyed each other's company. For so many years their relationship was at best civil, but something had changed. Unlike before, Eric found it easy to talk to her and decided to take a chance and share some things he always wanted to say to his mother. "Mom, I know I haven't been the best son, especially when I was growing up. I know it really hurt you when I stopped going to church. You gave me the silent treatment for almost a month. Then I got involved with the very people you told me to stay away from. I just want you to know how sorry I am that I was a disappointment to you."

"What?" Diane was surprised by her son's statement. "Is that what you think, that you were a disappointment to me. No, Eric, you were never a disappointment to me. I may have been disappointed in some of the things you did, but you were never a disappointment. I realize now how much I pushed church down your throat, and I can understand why you stopped going. After you left for college, I got tired of going to all those services myself." Eric couldn't believe it.

"Really, you . . . not at the church every night of the week. Tell me, Mom, what you did with all that free time? I sure hope you stayed out of trouble."

Eric was delighted to hear that his mother was finally getting a life. "I can assure you I stayed out of trouble, but there was a time . . . well never mind." All of a sudden Diane's happy-go-lucky demeanor changed. Her playful tone vanished, and she became serious. Eric was caught off guard by the switch. Anticipating a long drawn out religious discussion, Eric braced himself. "Eric, I need to talk to you about something." Diane's solemn attitude made Eric nervous.

"Sure, Mom. Is it something serious? You're not sick or anything, are you?" Eric sounded concerned.

Diane quickly responded, "No, I'm not sick, but it is serious, in a way. Son, let me start by saying that I love you, I always have." After a very long pause, she continued with her head down. Eric was stunned. His mother had always looked him in the eye when she spoke to him, but this time she did not. And why did she start off saying I love you, what was all of this about? Eric didn't have a clue. "This is hard for me to say, so please just bear with me. I have held this in for years, but I know this is the right time to tell you the truth." Eric was astonished by the fact that his mother wanted to confess something to him. She would have never, under any circumstances admit her mistakes. He concluded that perhaps he was adopted or something like that. Never in a million years would he have guessed what she was about to reveal.

"The truth about what? It's okay, Mom. Go ahead. Tell me." Eric felt knots in his stomach.

Diane sighed. "Well . . . I really don't know where to start. I guess I should start when your father and I broke up. When your father left me, you were about three years old. I was devastated. I moved back to my mother's house, and your grandmother was so glad. She needed us just as much as we needed her." After a very long pause, Diane continued, "I started going to the local bar down the street. At first I would go about once a week, but then I started going every night. I met a guy there who introduced me to marijuana and cocaine. After that I started using all kinds of drugs . . . you name it, I tried it. Eventually I became hooked on cocaine and . . . I hate to admit this, but I did a lot of things that I'm not proud of just to get another hit. I was out there, Son, really out there." Eric was shocked. His mother, the devoted church lady, was a drug addict who did anything to get a hit? He understood why she was always warning him to stay away from drugs. This information was about to ruin his macho image. He wanted to stop her, or at least ask for a moment to catch his breath, but he didn't interrupt her. "For the next two years, I was in and out of rehab. You were just getting ready to start kindergarten. As a matter of fact, I missed your first day at school because I was in rehab. I thank God for your grandmother. She was always there for you whenever I was out of pocket. Every time I came home from rehab and saw you, I felt so guilty. I constantly thought about what an awful mother I was, you deserved better. Here you are thinking you were a disappointment to me . . . no. I was a disappointment to you. I should have been a much better mother, but I wasn't. I was a terrible mother."

Eric was not only shocked by the fact that his mother had a drug problem, but he was flabbergasted when she said she wasn't a good mother. He sat there speechless. As he turned into the driveway, Diane insisted that he come inside so she could continue.

*"Continue? What more could she say?"* Eric's thoughts almost became verbal, but he kept his comments to himself. He wasn't sure how much more he could take. He opened the car door for his mother, and they went in the house, sat on the couch, and Diane picked up where she left off.

"I was in and out of the rehab center for the next two years or so. When you got older, I told you that I had a job that required a lot of traveling. I couldn't tell you the truth. I was too ashamed. I lied to you over and over again. Both your grandmother and I would stick with that story. I didn't want you to know where I really was. I was so tired of going back and forth to that facility. It just wasn't working for me. I had to do something else. I started going to church, the church you grew up in, with a friend. It was so easy for me to receive Jesus as my Savior. I really needed somebody to save me that I knew for sure. And from that day on, I was at church. To be honest with you, I went to church mostly just to keep out of the bar and away from the drug dealers that hung out there. I made you go to church because I didn't want you to turn out like me or your dad. I thought that if you went to church, it would keep you safe from the streets. I was really trying to protect you from that kind of life. That's the real reason why I was so disappointed when you decided to stop going."

*Eric was astonished that his mom had ulterior motives for hanging out at the church house.*

"When you started hanging out with those rough boys on the block, I was scared to death. I prayed that God would protect you. And right after that prayer, you got caught. At least when you were in juvenile hall you were off the streets. I didn't see it then, but now I believe God answered my prayers to keep you safe."

Eric nodded his head in agreement. "Yes, I can see how going to juvenile hall was God's way of getting me back on the right track. He certainly knows how to motivate a person to stay on the straight and narrow."

Hearing Eric acknowledge the ways of the Lord put a smile on Diane's face. "When you came back from juvenile hall, your grades in school were stellar. I always knew you had it in you. I am very proud of the man you've become."

"I know I made a lot of mistakes in raising you. Eric, I'm so sorry. I forced God and the Bible on you so much, I shouldn't have done that. Please forgive me. I didn't realize I was driving you away from the Lord. I love you so much please know that."

Eric listened intently to Diane's every word; he was astounded. He couldn't believe that his mother just confessed that she was a drug addicted and that she had made mistakes in raising him. He was barely able to speak. "Wow! Mom, that's a lot for me to take in."

Diane spoke but she couldn't look at her son; her tearful eyes were focused on the floor. "I know how shocking it must be to hear all of this. I'm sorry, but I have felt so guilty for so many years I had to tell you."

Eric was shocked but he was also relieved. Having this information cleared up so many things for him. He was also able to see how much his mother loved and cared for him. She forced God and church on him to keep him safe from the perilous dangers and bad influences that were prevalent in the neighborhood. He saw that his mother was protecting him to the best of her ability. He could no longer identify her as a religious fanatic. He now saw her mother as a caring, compassionate woman who did the best she could without a man in her life. Seeing her vulnerable and truthful soften Eric's heart toward his mom; he instantly forgave her.

"Do you remember when you got that trophy for winning the state debate competition. I think you were in the tenth grade. You could outtalk anybody, and whatever you said always made perfectly good sense." Eric treasured that complement from his mother. She did see him and acknowledged his accomplishments.

"Yes, I remember, I got the biggest trophy at the ceremony. I actually slept with that trophy for about a month before I finally put it up on the mantle. Mom, since you brought that up, I always wondered why you left right after the ceremony was over. I wanted you to stay for the reception so I could introduce you to my debate team coach, but I think you had to go to church for a meeting or something." Diane had left early for a good reason; she didn't want Eric to ever know where she had gone that day. But now she was going to tell her son the truth, the whole and nothing but the truth.

"No, no, I wasn't at church. I had a court date that day. Your father was contesting paying child support. As a matter of fact, I had many battles in court with your dad over supporting you. Your father would spend money on his clothes, shoes, cars, and women, but when it came to financially supporting you, he always claimed that he wasn't making any money. Believe me, your father made some serious under the table money. I had to fight him tooth and nail about paying child support. I didn't want you to know that. I never wanted you to know all that your daddy was into, or how much I was going through because of him." Eric suddenly had memories of gifts he received from his father while he was growing up. They seemed to somehow magically appear out of nowhere, especially on his birthday and also at Christmas. Eric's father may not have been present during special times in his life, but his gifts were always present and accounted for.

"What about all those birthday and Christmas gifts I got from Dad, you just made that up?"

Diane reluctantly replied, "Yes, I made all of those stories up. I didn't want you to be hurt."

"Mom, I would have given every one of those gifts back just to be with my dad." At that precise moment, Eric knew exactly how Cynthia felt when she told him that she wanted him, not just trinkets.

The more he thought about his non-supportive, absent, deadbeat father, the angrier Eric became. His anger had nothing to do with the confirmed fact his father never thought about him. He was mad that his mother endured years of emotional pain and financial hardship because of him. "Isn't Dad getting out of prison soon?" Eric calmly asked. Although he appeared cool, calm, and collected, inwardly Eric was furious.

"I think he'll be out in May. I'm not quite sure." Diane knew her son. Eric wanted to know when his father would be released so he could go off on him as soon as he hit the streets.

"Hum . . . can't wait to see him. I have some choice words for daddy dearest. I will never forgive him for what he's done to you. It's his fault that you got strung out on drugs." Eric was no longer calm.

Diane knew she had to talk loud and fast. "No, Eric, I was the one who chose to do drugs. It wasn't your father's fault. I take full responsibility for my own actions. That's one thing I learned in rehab, my sobriety depends on accepting responsibility for my own actions. I have forgiven your father. It took a while but I eventually forgave him. I hope you will find it in your heart to one day do the same." Eric couldn't believe the words coming out of his mother's mouth. She spoke as one who had learned from her mistakes. Her words were full of wisdom, and she spoke them with such confidence Eric was tempted to sarcastically ask, *Lady, are you my mother?* But he decided against it. Eric tried to remember ever hearing his mother speak negatively against his father; she never did. She never degraded his father, at least not in his presence. Eric had never noticed just how strong and classy his mother was. In fact, he was actually beginning to admire her.

"You can't change your father, and you can't change the fact that you got the short end of the stick when it comes to having a good father, but I always believed God kept him at a distance just so you wouldn't become like him."

Eric agreed with her statement, "You know, Mom, I said the same thing." Eric and his mother had finally seen eye to eye on something.

"I'm sure he regrets not being there for you. I know it. He just had too many issues of his own and chose not to deal with them. Son, God wants to bless you in so many ways, don't let unforgiveness block the favor of God in your life. Not letting go of bitterness and resentment only leads to your own detriment, it's not worth it. Think about the prayer of Jesus as he died on the Cross, 'Father, forgive them for they know not what they do.' Your father didn't know how his bad decisions would hurt you. Hum . . . I just thought about something. Your grandfather did the same thing to your father when he was growing up. He was abandoned by his father and never forgave him. Perhaps that's why his life turned out the way it did." Eric was stunned by this new and improved version of his mother. There was no harsh tone in her voice, she wasn't preachy and made no judgmental remarks, and she didn't have a holier-than-thou attitude.

"All right, Mom, I'll try to forgive him, but it won't be easy. Pray that God will give me the strength." Diane was thrilled that Eric had asked for prayer. She wanted to jump up and shout Hallelujah, right then and there, but she didn't want to frighten her son.

"I know, but God will give you the grace to do it. I will be praying." His mother reached out to hug him; they hadn't hugged in years. Eric had put a stop to all that excessive motherly affection around the age of fourteen. Diane knew that one day her little boy would no longer tolerate the hugs and kisses of his mommy. However, this time Eric did not hesitate at his mother's invitation for a hug.

"Mom, thanks for a wonderful evening. I am so glad we were able to really talk. So many things make sense now. Mom, I really appreciate all the sacrifices you made for me. I love you, Mom." They both stood, and Diane walked her son to the door.

"You're welcome, Son, I love you too . . . and thanks for not judging me."

Eric responded from a biblical stance, "Didn't Jesus say let him who is without sin cast the first stone?" Diane never thought she would see the day that her son would quote the Word of God. "Yes, you're right. Jesus did speak those words. Now try to remember them when you see your father."

"Okay, Mom, I'll try." Eric smirked. Eric walked away from his mother's house without the customary load of guilt. Diane closed the door, locked it, and shouted Glory Hallelujah!

She immediately called her prayer partner India. They had been praying and fasting that God would help Diane tell her son the truth; and that Eric could handle the truth. Both prayers were answered. Diane and India praised God together for hours.

Eric got in his car and immediately called Cynthia. He knew that she would be asleep, but he had to least leave a message. "Cyn, I have a major praise report. I'll give you details later. Let's just say for now God is still in the miracle working business. Love you, see you tomorrow."

Eric drove home thinking about the whole evening. He enjoyed the concert, was reconnected with his college buddy, and his mother made a serious confession to him. It was obvious to Eric that his mom was in a good church. She seemed so free. He couldn't wait to visit with Cynthia during an actual service. He then remembered that at his last session, coach prayed that God would do something miraculous for him. God had answered that prayer for sure. *"God really does move in mysterious ways,"* Eric thought to himself. Eric had heard that statement so many times from the "religious" Diane. However this time, for Eric it was no longer a religious cliché; it was a fact.

# Chapter 23

When Eric woke up, he wasn't sure if what happened last night was real or just a very vivid dream. The whole experience was definitely surreal, but the sense of contentment he felt confirmed that last night was no dream. This feeling of fulfillment had nothing to do with personal accomplishments, a job promotion, or accolades from coworkers. The things Eric believed would bring him satisfaction fell short when compared to God's priceless blessings. God poured into his life things that money could never buy. He was establishing an intimate relationship with God, he had a whole new wonderful relationship with his mother, he was reconnected to his friend Michael after twenty years, and his relationship with Cynthia was better than ever. All of these things were priceless.

Sunday was Eric and Cynthia's hang out day that always began with going out to breakfast. He couldn't wait to share his incredible story with her. When he arrived at her house, Cynthia opened the door with the most beautiful smile on her face. They kissed as Eric entered. He held Cynthia in his arms and wasn't about to let her go until she broke loose from his embrace. Cynthia took his hand and escorted him to the beautifully adorned dining room table. Eric sat down in amazement. "I thought we'd have our Sunday morning breakfast here. Everything is ready. I just have to take the homemade biscuits out of the oven." Cynthia gracefully whisked off into the kitchen. Eric was stunned and speechless. After putting the food on the table, Cynthia handed him a glass of mimosa, lifted up her glass and asked Eric to do the honors. "Wow, baby, wha"s really going on! You never cook. This is incredible sweetness, thank you." He got up and gave her a tender kiss. "Here's to my amazing, beautiful, sweet, and adorable woman, Cynthia. And to our awesome, magnificent heavenly Father, who has done wonders in our life's and our relationship" They clicked glasses, took a sip and sat down to eat. "Okay, Eric,"m all ears. Tell me what happened, and don't leave anything out" Eric told his incredible testimony, and as instructed, he didn't leave anything out.

# Chapter 24

After what he considered to be one of the best weekends of his life, Eric woke up Monday morning, refreshed and ready to get back to the grindstone. He scheduled his appointment with coach, bright and early and planned to go into work after his session. Sharing all of this wonderful news with coach was the perfect way to cap off an incredible weekend. On the way to his session, Eric picked up a token of his appreciation to coach for her wisdom and for reigniting his relationship with God and with Cynthia. Eric walked into coach's office and handed her a bouquet of multicolored roses.

ERIC: These are for you. I had to say thank you in a tangible way.

*Coach couldn't remember the last time she had received flowers from a man. She received them with bright eyes and a beautiful smile. Eric couldn't help but notice just how beautiful coach was. He wasn't sure of her age, he guessed that she was probably in her fifties. Of course he would never ask how old she was, but whatever her age, she was very attractive. Eric wondered but again, wouldn't dare ask, if there was a man in her life.*

COACH: Oh! Wow! Thank you, Eric, how thoughtful of you. I assume everything went well on Saturday.

*As one who believed in taking time to stop and smell the roses, coach took a whiff of the fragrant flowers before putting them in a vase.*

ERIC: Saturday was miraculous in so many ways. The whole weekend was just great!

COACH: All right, let's pray and get started. I can't wait to hear what happened.

Lord, thank you for moving so mightily in Eric's life. We, Eric and I, rejoice together in your goodness toward us. Open our hearts today to receive your appointed blessings for this session. We give you honor and glory, forever. Amen.

Whew, I know this is going to be good. All right, Eric, go ahead.

ERIC: Will let me start off by saying thank you Jesus because without God none of this would have ever happened, none of it. I'll start with my reflection paper. You were right, I really did get a lot out of the assignment. It really put me in a whole different place with God. I don't want to leave anything out so I'll just read my paper.

COACH: Sounds good.

*As Eric read his paper, my heart was leaping for joy. I laughed when he described the picture of Adam and Eve being expelled from the garden. I knew exactly what he was talking about; I had that same children's bible. He's getting it. He no longer viewed God as a nebulous cosmic enforcer but as a concerned loving Father. When he finished reading, I just sat there in amazement.*

ERIC: Well, what do you think?

COACH: To tell you the truth, I'm speechless.

ERIC: Well since you're speechless I'll keep talking. I had an extraordinary experience with my mother. She confessed a major secret to me. My mother was once hooked on drugs. With her confession a lot of things make sense to me now…oh, one more thing. My best friend from college, who I haven't seen in years just moved to the city and goes to my mother's church.

COACH: Showers of Blessings, amazing. Isn't God amazing!

ERIC: Yes, he is!

# Chapter 25

After a wonderful weekend and another great session with coach, Eric headed to work rejuvenated. Because of several new clients, the workload for his team was going to be extremely heavy for the next two months. Everyone on the team was assigned a specific task, and it was imperative that everyone pull his own weight. Even though his work schedule would be horrendous, Eric had always been one who actually thrived when the pressure was on. Eric arrived just in time for the final preplanning meeting. The final instructions were given, and Eric was ready for the challenge, or so he thought. Robert dismissed the meeting and asked that everyone give a update on their progress before the end of the day.

As soon as I got to my desk, Robert came in my office, closed the door, and sheepishly started asking the most mundane questions about the project. It took everything I had to keep all sarcastic remarks in my head only. For a whole hour Robert asked one stupid question after another, he made several ridiculous suggestions, and went on and on repeating the same thing over and over again. I did pretty well keeping it all together until Robert informed me that he would return to my office after lunch to get more insight. I went *off!* Every suppressed mocking comment came flying out of my mouth with force. In the midst of my rampage it dawned on me, that I had just called my boss an incompetent piece of you know what. I was just about to apologize for my behavior, but it was too late. Robert stormed out and headed straight to Mr. Randle's office.

At the end of the day while everyone gathered into the conference room to give their updates, I was asked to report to Mr. Randle. "Eric, come in and have a seat." Mr. Randle glared from his glasses and with a firm look, he handed me a memo. "This is the information regarding the upcoming anger management workshop. I want you there or you will be terminated." Eric sat there stunned for a moment and tried to give a reasonable explanation for his outburst.

"Being the fair man that you are, Mr. Randle, I'm sure you want to hear my side of the story." Eric was shocked and angry at Mr. Randle's answer. "No, there is no need for further discussion. Robert has told me all I need to know. You just make sure you're at the very next workshop or else!" *"Or else what, you'll fire me. Go ahead I was about to quit anyway."* Eric managed to keep his thoughts to himself. Instead he assured Mr. Randle that he would attend and walked out before another word was said. Eric hated ultimatums and would have quit, but leaving a good paying job in the middle of a recession made his decision easy. As soon as he got back to his desk, he called and registered for the next anger management workshop. For the rest of the day, Eric thought it best to avoid Robert and hoped that Robert had enough sense to stay away from him.

Eric left the office at 9:00 p.m., which was very late for him. As soon as he got home, he headed straight to the refrigerator, grabbed a can of beer, and tried to erase the stress of the day. After drinking two cold cans of beer back to back, Eric had no relief. His blissful feelings from the perfect weekend had been replaced with rage as thoughts of not getting Robert's position began to haunt him once again. He started to pour himself a shot of tequila, but changed his mind. There was another urge that suddenly rose up inside of him; the intensity was undeniable. Eric was surprised by the strong promptings he felt to pray. So he did.

"Dear God, I know that I shouldn't have gone off on Robert like that, but he had it coming . . . He . . . he . . . No, let me take responsibility for my own actions. I'm not trying to do the blame game thing like Adam. Lord, I am coming to you with the good, the bad, and the ugly in my life. I guess I really need to go to that anger management workshop. I will no longer deny that I need to deal with this. I'm going to go and trust you. I remember a scripture that says that you order my footsteps. So I will go with the thought that you are sending me there. Maybe this class is the next step toward the abundant life that Jesus promised me. Amen."

§

Regardless of the drama at work, Eric was looking forward to going to the game with Michael. The Knicks and Celtics game was tonight, and when Michael called offering the ticket to Eric, of course he accepted. No man in his right mind would ever turn down an offer like that. Besides, going to the basketball game was the perfect diversion for Eric. The game was close, but the Knicks managed to win 104-101. "Now that was a game. Man, this is just what I needed. Why don't we head over to the sports bar and play a few games of pool like we always did after a good game. Are you up to the challenge?"

Eric knew Michael would never back away from a challenge. "Please, all that weed smoking must have tampered with your memory." Michael had never smoked, but back in the day, Eric was known as a cannabis connoisseur.

"When have I ever backed down to one of your pitiful challenges." Eric and Michael played pool and reminisced about their escapades. Michael clearly remembered many things, but Eric's memories were a bit foggy.

"Please tell me that you put that stuff down. It seems like you only have two or three long-term memory cells left in that brain of yours," Michael taunted Eric and showed no mercy.

"I refuse to answer that question without my lawyer present." Eric laughed and confessed that he had stopped the weed smoking several years ago.

After three games of pool, Michael maintained his legacy as being the college pool shark. Eric refused to play another game and insisted that it was time to get something to eat. The two friends ate and brought each other up to speed regarding their current lives. Michael had been married for six years and spoke of his wife as if they were still newlyweds. He was excited that the baby was due in just six more weeks. Eric knew that Michael would make an excellent father; the kind of dad Eric always wanted. His career was thriving, and Michael was transferred to New York to set up new offices for the computer company he worked for. As he talked, Michael gave God all the glory for his career, his wife, and his soon-to-be-born baby boy.

"Mike, how did you make the decision to get married? I have a special lady in my life, and I'm trying to decide if I'm ready to get married. I've been putting it off for a while, but I believe that Cynthia is the one for me. I have to say that I'm encouraged by the fact that you and Denise are still enjoying each other after six years." Eric had never talked about the subject of marriage to anyone other than Cynthia. He had always valued Michael's opinion and was opened to any advice he had to offer. Michael was glad that Eric, the playboy of NYU, had finally found a woman who had captured his heart.

"I can't wait to meet Cynthia. She must be a very special lady. Okay, so let me tell you, Denise and I met right after college. After three years of dating, we broke up for some reason, but after about a year of being apart, we somehow made it back to each other. I did have some apprehensions at first about getting married, but I realized that my life works better with Denise in it." He went on to say that even though they had rough patches along the way, they grew closer during those times. Their marriage became stronger with each hardship they encountered. When he said that, Eric thought about Cynthia and how their relationship had grown stronger over the past year. Eric told Michael about Cynthia, the sessions with the coach, his new found relationship with God, and the mandated anger management class. They both laughed.

"None of our friends would ever believe that I finally got a grip on my wild side. I must confess I was out of control most of the time. I guess I have a little more wildness to deal with."

"Yes, but I think our friends would be more surprised to hear you talking about God, and they would have never guessed that we reconnected in a church," Eric agreed. Michael was glad to hear that Eric had changed his ways. "You were always up in somebody's face. I think you still owe me some money for the last time I bailed you out of jail for unruly conduct. Do you remember that?"

"Yes, I do." Eric reached in his pocket and put a hundred-dollar bill on the table. "I think this should cover it." Michael refused to take the money, but Eric insistent. "Just look at it as a love offering for your consistent ministry to me. I have thought about the spiritual impact you have had on my life and that's priceless. Take it and go buy a present for the baby something special from his uncle Eric."

"All right, since you put it that way." Michael put the money in his pocket, and the two friends promised that they would get together real soon. Spending time with Michael was exactly what Eric needed.

# Chapter 26

## Control Your Anger Before It Controls You An Anger Management Workshop

### Anger is only one letter short of danger . . . unknown

Eric wasn't looking forward to attending the anger management workshop; it was all day, and he could think of better things to do on such a beautiful Saturday. Sitting in a workshop all day wasn't on his things-to-do list. However, he had to make it his number one priority if he wanted to remain employed. Even though Mr. Randle didn't say it was mandated, he attached a serious ultimatum so to Eric it was mandated. "All I know is I'd better walk out of here with my certification of completion or else. So many people are losing their jobs, I should be grateful that I still have one."

Eric arrived minutes before the workshop began. As he scanned the room looking for the best place to sit, he noticed several people he had worked with before. Most of them were also turned down for a promotion; apparently, he wasn't the only one who felt slighted and had no problem letting it be known. "There goes that loud mouth Ronald. They transferred me from that team just in the nick of time. Like my father always used to say, 'that guy is cruzin' for a bruisin' and I would have no problem giving him some bruises. And there goes Ms. Janet, trying to hide behind a magazine. She thinks she's all that, but she's the only one who thinks it." Eric didn't know it but several people in the room had similar thoughts about him. It took a while, but Eric was able to find a seat far away from those who knew him.

The workshop began as Mrs. Jackson, the anger management guru, introduced herself. Right off the bat, she disclosed that the number one reason that people are unable to make it up the corporate ladder in this company revolves around anger management issues. The regional managers place working well with others over a person's sheer ability to get the job done. In this business, teamwork is essential, and the ability to get the job done with the team still intact was the number one priority in getting promoted. Eric paid closer attention; Coach told him to always be open to hear from God in unlikely places. Eric believed this could be one of those places.

Ms. Jackson explained that anger is a completely normal human emotion that must be expressed, but in healthy ways. Unexpressed anger can cause conditions such as hypertension, high blood pressure, or depression. Others may tend to exaggerate their emotions and become explosive. Some people use anger as a way to avoid feeling hurt, but that doesn't mean the hurt goes away. While others rather than confronting people directly will use passive-aggressive behavior to get their point across. This type of behavior includes things like, giving the silent treatment, withholding sex, affection, or compliments. Intentionally being late or gossiping also indicate passive-aggressive tendencies. However, indirect actions of anger against someone will never bring resolution and will perpetuate dysfunctional relationship patterns. Other inappropriate ways of expressing anger include constantly putting others down, criticizing, being judgmental, making cynical comments, and the use of sarcastic humor. All of these behaviors are disguised forms of anger. Angry people tend to demand things: fairness, appreciation, agreement, or willingness to do things their way. Everyone wants these things, and we are all hurt and disappointed when we don't get them, but angry people demand them, and when their demands aren't met, their disappointment becomes anger. In a working environment, anger can alienate people who might otherwise be willing to work with you. As Ms. Jackson was talking, no one dared to look around. Everyone, including Eric, sat frozen, staring straight ahead. She was stepping on everyone's toes, Eric's in particular.

Hurtful childhood events or subconscious memories of traumatic experiences can also trigger anger that is still buried within. For instance, the tone in which your boss speaks may irritate you and feelings of anger begin to slowly emerge. And yet you have no idea that subconsciously his tone reminds you of your father's tone when he scolded you as a child. *"How well do you think this person will respond if reprimanded by his boss?"* Eric thought about his anger toward his father and wondered how many subconscious grenades were safely tucked away in his suppressed memories.

The aim is not to suppress anger but convert it into constructive behavior. Participation in this workshop will give you ways to express anger in a healthy manner, even if you are provoked. You will learn effective coping behaviors to stop anger from escalating and interpersonal relationship skills that will help in resolving conflicts. Eric tried not to smirk at her lofty expectations and thought, *"Robert provokes me with his stupidity, and after about five idiotic statements, my anger level goes from three to ten in a split second. What they need to do is put Robert's ass in an all day workshop on how not to be so stupid, then I wouldn't be so angry. And if anyone provokes me intentionally, there is absolutely nothing that Ms. Jackson could come up with to curtail my anger. That would be one conflict that would never be resolved."*

The second part of the workshop consisted of skits that portrayed everything that had been mentioned in the lecture. After each skit, we were to write out any situation in which we displayed the type of unhealthy anger expressions portrayed in the vignettes. I easily identified myself in the first skit. A couple having an argument, and the man walked and didn't come home for hours. And when he did return, neither one of them talked about what caused the disagreement in the first place. Cynthia and I had done that many times in our relationship. I thought that if I just walked away and disappeared for a while, I was handling my anger in a healthy way, surely that was a healthier decision than going postal on somebody. I believed that if I removed myself from the scene, I was defusing the inevitable destructive blow up. But disappearing and just holding in the rage doesn't extinguish the fuse. Usually the explosion would be delayed or released in another context that had nothing to do with the original source of my angst. I would disappear without a word and would eventually return without a word as to why I left in the first place. I can see how this behavior doesn't resolve anything.

Watching the portrayal of passive-aggressive behavior also got to me. I do that all the time. As a matter of fact, that's exactly what I did after our first session with the coach. I was so mad at Cynthia that I drove home like a bat out of hell, just to irritate her. I didn't talk about why I was so angry, but I literally drove like a mad man.

The next skit centered around disrespecting others with snide remarks and using sarcastic humor. I was sitting a couple of rows behind one of the victims of my brutal, sarcastic assaults. He did tell another coworker that he would never work with me again. Poor guy, I had humiliated him, no doubt about that. I probably should apologize to him before the day is over.

The skit that bothered me the most was of a child being neglected by his father. That one hit too close to home. But thanks to coach, I already realized that a lot of my anger actually stemmed from being disappointed by my dad's consistent stream of broken promises. I'd probably be fighting off tears right now if I hadn't had those sessions.

In the last sketch, a healthy looking woman in her early forties was being examined by her doctor. She complained of various ailments and severe insomnia. She was going through a divorce. She was angry about her situation and was completely stressed out. The doctor also recommended that she see a psychologist.

*I had no idea that anger could have such a traumatic effect on the body. I work out physically, and I'm getting an internal workout with coach. If everyone who took the time to work on their physical would take time to deal with this stuff, people wouldn't be so crazy. It's like everybody's slowly but surely losing their minds all together. Humm, I plan to keep mine in tack and well-functioning at all times.*

The last segment of the workshop was in a breakout format allowing for role playing and discussion. The topics offered were: Developing Better Communication Skills, How to Really Relax, The Value of Spiritual Disciplines, Work It Out: How Physical Exercise Regulates Anger, and last but not least, my favorite by far, Count To 10 and Reel It In: How To Stay Out of This Mandated Workshop.

I have always been good at achieving my goals. Whatever issues I have I'll just treat them like goals to accomplish. Let's see what else can I say? Well, by the time he walked out of the workshop, Eric had almost turned into a self-help guru himself. He soaked up that information like a sponge because he saw it as the Lord sending him more wisdom for personal growth. Coach made it very clear that what she does is only a segment of the becoming whole process. Coach explained that since we are multidimensional as human beings, our healing and the processes thereby will also be multidimensional.

Also we must understand that the process is ongoing, can activate at any time, can occur simultaneously on various levels, involves intense times of pain but will result in a tremendous amount of freedom and personal fortitude. The priceless benefits can't be fathomed, and yet they will never be obtained if the process is resisted. It will require faith, courage, and patience to persevere, but it will be well worth it. That coach is something else. She can really break it down. She says we all need a spirit, soul, and body tune up every now and then. Boy, do I get it. Hate to admit it, but I'm so glad Cynthia put her foot down on this one; it's all good.

As soon as the workshop was over, Eric headed for the car. The phone was already ringing as he opened the door. He already knew it was Cynthia being nosy. Eric called her back, "Sweetness, I know you want to know what I learned today. All I will say for now is actions speak louder than words and that's all you need to know." Cynthia held the receiver to her ear with her mouth wide open. She knew Eric all too well, if he had that "I'm the man tone in his voice," she knew he meant what he was saying. When he spoke like that he wasn't mean or angry, he just meant it. So Cynthia did the wisest thing she could do, she changed the subject. However, from that point on Cynthia was anticipating seeing the actions Eric alluded to. And like most women, Cynthia would remember his words, verbatim for a very, very long time.

§

For the next two months, Eric faithfully put his anger management techniques into action. It took a while for him to make the necessary adjustments, but with each day he made progress. Robert was the same annoying boss as he had always been. He hadn't changed, but Eric had. After a few months, everyone on the team noticed the transformation but would never comment on it out loud. They weren't exactly sure how long this new and improved version of Eric would last.

Over time Eric remained consistent and was chosen to negotiate a contract with a group of investors who were interested in purchasing a hotel in Maui. Eric was shocked that the recommendation had come from Robert. This time instead of feeling like he deserved the assignment, Eric gave all the glory to God. He was scheduled to leave in three days. That night, he and Cynthia went out for a celebratory dinner and anticipated another celebration when he return with a contract.

§

On the flight to Maui, Eric thought about the changes in his life, thanks to his time with the coach. A wonderful change had indeed come over him. Eric prayed a prayer of thanksgiving and asked God to be with him during his entire trip. Coming home with this contract would be the most lucrative deal of his career and would open many doors of opportunity for him. This one meeting could literally change his whole life. Eric felt confident but not arrogant; he was humbled by the opportunity but not prideful. Sitting in first class, looking out of the window, mesmerized by the beautiful ocean, and headed for one of his favorite vacation spots, Eric's heart filled with worship to the Lord. He decided that with this bonus, he would give a tithe to his mother's church; he was so grateful. Words from a hymn flooded his mind. He was glad that no one was sitting next to him because it gave him the freedom to sing softly, out loud.

*O Lord, my god, when I in awesome wonder, consider all the works thy hand hath made. I see the stars, I hear the mighty thunder, thy power throughout the universe displayed Then sings my soul, My Savior God, to Thee, How great Thou art! How great Thou art! Then sings my soul, My Savior God, to Thee, How great Thou art! How great Thou art!*

He didn't remember the second verse, so he sang the first verse and refrain over and over until he fell asleep. He woke up to the announcement that the plane was preparing to land. The stewardess welcomed the passengers to Maui and extended a hearty aloha. As soon as Eric walked off the plane, he knew that this was his appointed time. He had prepared himself for this season. He was ready to receive all that God had for him. As he pondered these things another song arose from his heart, "To God Be The Glory, for the Things He has done."

# Chapter 27

When Eric and I first came to see coach, we blamed each other for our problems. But when we took the time to really look at ourselves individually, we came to the startling conclusion that we both had faults. We both needed and allowed healing to take place within our own souls. As a result our relationship naturally became better over time.

Eric's been traveling a lot on business. I miss him, but I no longer feel that deep empty pain of loneliness. I can't believe it; it's like my own personal miracle. Thank you, Jesus! I'm okay. I'm really okay. Sometimes it's just hard to believe. I am so different, I have to get use to the new me. I'm telling the truth; sometimes I have to pinch myself to make sure it's still me. I'm stronger (spirit, soul, and body) and happier than I have been in my whole life. And in all of this, what shocks me the most is that this fulfillment came, not from a husband, but from my Father God.

I was always looking for "the one" who would love me forever. I never considered that God would be "the one." Like the knight in shining armor (who I knew one day would come for me) he rescued me. My soul was wounded, trapped under the rubble of childhood emotional scars. The depth of this brokenness, the very core of my personhood . . . All the kings' horses and all the kings' men couldn't put Cynthia together again, but God could and did. Coach once told me that I had a lot of faith. I don't know about that. Certainly, I have grown in the faith department, I just didn't give up. I refused to let the pain of my past continue block the brightness of my future.

As I gained knowledge concerning how much God loves me, I am also learning how to love myself. One day while I was cleaning out my closet, the

Holy Spirit began to reveal something so powerful to me. Over the years I had purchased so many designer things, and I really should be embarrassed, it's just ridiculous. Anyway, I was carefully hanging up my clothes this thought came to me out of nowhere, . . . "If you can understand the value of your designer-labeled outfits and expensive shoes by taking such good care of them, why won't you do that for you. Start treating yourself with the same loving care as you do for your clothes and shoes. After all, you are more valuable than your whole wardrobe put together. Don't wait for a man to make you feel special. You are already special, start treating and conducting yourself as such. As a matter of fact, you're priceless because I, the master designer created you." God was affirming my worth and value to him, using the example of designer clothes, the very thing I could relate too, to get his point across. I love it when he does that. That impression was so powerful I almost passed out right there in my closet.

I remember hearing someone say that if you take one step God would take two. No, it's more like he'll take gigantic leaps and bounds into places I would not and could not go. His giant steps brought healing to inaccessible places in my soul. I have now moved beyond the harmful gravitational pull of my internal faults. And now, I don't overspend, I don't over work and I have gained appreciation for life's little pleasures. I started exercising and lost 15 lbs, almost effortlessly. I can even go out of the house with no makeup, wearing sweats and dirty tennis shoes.

Although I have gone through a lot of emotional healing, at times I am still mindful of the vulnerable young places of myself. But, now when I hear that faint cry of "Who's going to love me now?" or if I feel the emptiness or panicky, I hasten to God's throne. By discovering the power of simple prayers and meditating in the Word, I am growing in the relationship that matters the most. My relationship with God! I spend time with God throughout the day in various ways. I see him in nature, I hear him in music, and most importantly I have learned how to be still in bask in his presence. No words need be spoken, I'm just being . . . with him.

God saw my need for love and all the mistakes I made trying to get love, but the Lord didn't judge or condemn me. He looked beyond my faults, saw my real need and met the need.

Like a time released medication for the soul, the Lord will heal me as often as needed. By the power of his perfecting love, he has and will continue to heal me from fear, guilt, shame and whatever else that comes up.

And for this . . . All of this . . . Lord, I give you praise!

# Chapter 28

When Eric arrived in Maui, it was close to dusk. He was glad that it didn't take long for him to get his luggage. Whenever he came to Maui, he always rented a red convertible. The warm tropical breeze, beautiful blue sky, and magnificent shoreline could only be fully appreciated driving slowly with the top down. However, this time he was in a hurry. After checking into the hotel, Eric went straight to his ocean-view suite. He changed his clothes, poured a glass of wine, and headed for the balcony. He had made it just in time to watch the sunset. Sunsets in Maui are exquisite, and he didn't want to miss one moment. Unlike Cynthia, Eric knew how to relax, and watching the sunsets of Maui was a relaxation ritual for him since his first visit to the island. Mesmerized by the awesome display of beauty in the sky, Eric acknowledged the awesome artistry of God. Giving reverence to him came naturally in a setting such as this. The vibrant colors of lavender, red, purple, and gold were spectacular declarations of God's glory.

Basking in the beauty of the sunset, Eric smiled as he thought of another one of God's beautiful creations, his Cynthia. Eric remembered when they were introduced. That was a wonderful night. They talked, danced, flirted, and laughed all night. The first time he laid eyes on Cynthia, she was gorgeous and her smile was captivating, just like the beauty of the sunset. After a wonderful evening with Cynthia, Eric wasn't sure if he should see her again. Not because he didn't want to, but because he knew she was special. He already had at least three women as sexual play toys, and he knew that Cynthia was not to be played with. He asked for her number but wasn't sure if he would call. But the next day he called. He couldn't help it, she was irresistible. As he got to know her better, Eric realized how being with Cynthia brought out the best in him.

After dating for only two months, Eric knew that Cynthia was who he wanted and needed in his life, but of course he kept that information to himself. Slowly but surely, he skillfully maneuvered his three bed buddies out of his life; he was ready for a change. And now five years later, Eric was ready to make another change.

*Cynthia would love this sunset. She should be sitting right here with me. Hum . . . a honeymoon in Maui would be nice. Wait a minute, did I say honeymoon? I'm thinking about a honeymoon? Me!* Eric shocked himself with that thought, but the more he thought about it, "Marriage is not to be entered into lightly, but reverently, advisedly, and soberly." Eric was sober in his thinking; he had be advised through his sessions with the coach and talking to Michael about the reality of being married. But most importantly, he had reestablished his relationship with God. He was ready to reverently enter into the divine covenant of marriage, and he was happy. Last year, when he proposed, it was out of obligation. But now, exactly a year later, he was ready to propose from and with his whole heart.

*Okay Lord, I'm ready. Let's do this. Thank you for bringing Cynthia into my life.*

*Cynthia's suitable for me. She fits me; she's my rib all right. She is the one to walk by my side through life, till death do us part. I want to make Cynthia happy. She deserves it, and I know what will make her happy. This time I'm giving her all of me; not part of me bearing expensive trinkets. And then I'll reintroduce the trinkets and spoil her with all that I desire to give. I already know that a happy woman will have no problem keeping her man happy.*

Last year, when Cynthia broke off the engagement, she gave the ring back. Eric concluded that it was time to put the ring back where it belonged, on Cynthia's finger. Since he would be getting a sizeable bonus from this deal, he wanted to add a few more karats in the center stone and more baguettes on the wedding band. He also thought that the perfect wedding gift for her would be a matching baguette diamond bracelet.

Before going to bed, Eric called Cynthia to pray with her concerning his presentation. They acknowledged and gave thanks to the Lord for all the blessings that were flowing into their relationship. They prayed for God's divine favor upon Eric as he gave his presentation. They even prayed and thanked God for the coach. She was the one who taught them the value of simple prayers. They wanted God to bless her with the very thing she needed the most. They didn't know what it was, but they knew God did.

§

By the end of the next day, Eric had closed the deal and had a signed contract in his briefcase. Of course, he couldn't wait to give Cynthia the exciting news. God certainly answered their prayers. At that instant, the Holy Spirit brought to Eric's memory a scripture Michael shared with him the night of the game, "He who finds a wife finds a good thing and obtains favor from the Lord." Eric heard what the Holy Spirit was saying loud and clear. "Cynthia is my good thing, my wife. I do have more of God's favor in my life when she's in it. This signed contract definitely confirms that. Besides that, the thought of her being with someone else would haunt me for the rest of my life."

I called Cynthia and gave her the good news. She was so proud of me. Growing up, I always wanted my mom to be proud of me like that. It's like God is using Cynthia's love to heal me from what I didn't get back then. Now that's real deep! I'm starting to sound like the coach.

After talking to Cynthia, Eric went and talked to the hotel honeymoon consultant.

*Valentine's Day was just around the corner, and Eric had a lot do in just a few short weeks.*

# Chapter 29

Eric knew his schedule would be hectic as soon as he returned from his business trip. Eric was going to be busy all right, but not from his job. All of his thoughts centered on planning how he would propose to Cynthia. He had so much to accomplish in just a few days. He called Cynthia and explained that he was going to be extremely busy and would not be able to see her until Valentine's Day. He promised that they would go and celebrate getting the contract and that he had a special Valentine gift for her. Cynthia understood; she knew that a business transaction such as this required a lot of detailed work. She assured him it was okay and hung up the phone with a smile on her face. *"A special Valentine's Day gift . . . I hope it's the tiffany necklace that matches my bracelet."*

Eric thought of his healing journey that led him to this moment. He wanted that night to serve as a testimonial to God who blessed him with such a precious, invaluable gift, his soon-to-be wife. He wanted this night to be exceptional, one that Cynthia would treasure forever.

He began writing down his thoughts and made detailed plans for what he wanted. Eric called and spoke with Vincent, the maître d' at Cynthia's favorite restaurant regarding his plans for the evening. Vincent knew exactly who Eric and Cynthia were. He made it a point to remember them because Eric would always leave a sizable tip, especially for him. Eric wanted his same table, the one by the window with the panoramic view of the city. Cynthia's eyes always sparkled with delight by the glistening city lights. There were live musician that played softly in the dining area: piano, harp, and violin. Every night the musicians would rotate. Vincent informed him that on that night the harpist would be playing. Eric asked if she could be positioned near their table. As soon as they were seated, the waiter was to

147

come with a bottle of Dom Pérignon Rosé 1995. Eric didn't flinch when he was informed that the champagne was $350 a bottle. As the champagne was being poured, he wanted the flower lady to come and give him a single long stem red rose.

Vincent assured Eric that every one of his request would be done with excellence.

The next on his list was the engagement ring. Eric took the original platinum engagement ring he had bought for Cynthia last year back to the jewelers. He had the ¾ carat center stone replaced with a flawless D, two-carat stone. He had the wedding band engraved with his and Cynthia's initials along with the inscription "A Love Affair for Life." Just to be sure that the rings would be ready on time, he paid the additional fee for special rush jobs.

Eric then arranged for two deliveries to arrive at Cynthia's house. The first delivery would come at 11:00 a.m. and the second at noon. The first gift was a combo gift pack that included: a bouquet of 24 sixteen-inch red roses, a premium Day Spa gift certificate, and a box of chocolates. The second delivery was a light silk, short length, red evening dress. The Sunday before leaving for his business trip, he and Cynthia went window shopping. Eric knew that since it was getting close to Valentine's Day Cynthia was going to start dropping subtle hints of what she wanted. He made it a point to act like he wasn't paying attention, but he always did.

§

On Saturday morning, Eric called and wished Cynthia a happy Valentine's Day and gave strict instructions that she was not to leave the house before noon.

At exactly 11:00 a.m., the first delivery was made. Cynthia was elated with the roses, spa trip, and her favorite chocolates. She cried as she read the card. "Cynthia, you are my gift, my special angel, and I will cherish you forever. I love you, baby." Eric. At noon the second delivery was made. Cynthia took her time to admire the beautifully wrapped box before opening it.

She slowly opened the box. She screamed and laughed for joy; it was the dress she had shown to Eric last week. The card read "To my sweetness. You thought I wasn't paying attention to what you wanted. Let me assure you, baby, I always will. I want you to wear this tonight. You are going to be the most beautiful, sexiest woman in the room, just like when I first laid eyes on you. Can't wait to be with you my love." Eric.

Cynthia just stood there in awe. Her classy man was pulling out the "big guns." She didn't get the necklace, but she didn't even miss it. Cynthia went to the beauty salon floating on air. It took all afternoon, but her hair, nails, and feet were perfect. She had a facial and brows waxed. Her man was giving her his best, and she was going to make him proud to have her on his arm.

Promptly at 8:00 p.m. Eric arrived looking like he had just stepped out of the latest *GQ* magazine. Cynthia embraced and kissed him, thanking him for each gift. "Oh, you are so welcome, my love. You look absolutely stunning. That dress fits just right in all the right places. You are so beautiful, sexy, and irresistible, and I have one more trinket for you." He then pulled the noteworthy blue bag from around his back. She knew it was the necklace. Before she even opened the gift, Cynthia gave him the most passionate kiss she could. Like never before, Eric could feel the depth of her love for him. His heart was now open to give and receive love from a whole place. He didn't know he could love anyone that deeply. But the damn that was assigned to block him from giving and receiving love had burst. He was in love, really in love. The bond between them had become much stronger; it was undeniable, and they both knew it.

Eric escorted Cynthia to the limousine. Up until now, she thought Eric drove his car. She couldn't hold back the tears when she saw the driver and the beautiful limo awaiting them. Eric helped her into the car, made sure she was comfortable, and handed her a crystal wine glass. He could barely pour the wine because his woman was all over him. He loved the fact that she was so affectionate. And so was he, they couldn't keep their hands off each other. Finally, he poured the wine and performed the celebratory toasting ritual they had devised on their first date. With glasses raised, Cynthia went first. "To my wonderful man who I love completely. I am so proud of you. You said you were going to get that contract and you did. Here's to you, my love." They clicked glasses, took a sip, and raised them again. It was Eric's turn. "To you, my sweet, sexy, and beautiful gift from God. I promise you that I will always treat you exactly as that . . . my exquisite gift." They clicked glasses, took another sip, and continued to shower each other with affection, pure and sweet. The passionate chemistry between them was undeniable from the start. He told her how much he respected her for not becoming part of his sexual harem; he had never had a relationship that didn't go straight to the bedroom. Cynthia wasn't having that. They took time to develop a good solid friendship first. Of course, Eric kept messing around with her to wear down her resistance. And when that day finally came, they knew there would be no problems in the bedroom, no problems at all. Of course, Eric brought up the day she called his gifts trinkets. They laughed as he pointed out each trinket she was wearing. They also found humor in every single one of their breakups over the past five years and concluded that they could no longer fight the force that always pulled them back together; it was bigger than both of them.

As the Limo came to a stop, Eric said to Cynthia before opening the door, "Cynthia, we have an amazing relationship. We were meant to be together." He softly kissed her lips, and before she could say a word, Eric was out of the car, reaching for her left hand. As he gently pulled her out of the limo, he took the ring out of his pocket, and with a smooth move, he slipped the ring on her finger. "Cynthia, I'm ready to take the next step. Let's continue this amazing journey together as husband and wife. I love you and would be honored to have you for my wife. Marry me, my sweetness." Cynthia was in complete utter awe and overwhelmed with pure joy. She was laughing and crying at the same time. She didn't care about ruining her makeup, hair, or anything else.

She could barely speak. "Yes, yes, yes, I will marry you, Eric. *Yes!*" They kissed and held each other tightly for at least ten minutes.

Eric draped her arm over his. "As many times as we have been here to celebrate special occasions, I want you to now walk into this place, the place of our first date as my fiancée, shall we?"

"Yes, we shall," Cynthia replied. They had a natural, graceful elegance about them that attested to the fact that they belonged together. They both had style, class, and charm as individuals, and together, they looked like royalty.

Cynthia kissed Eric on the cheek and went to the restroom to reapply her makeup. Eric went over to see Vincent to make sure everything was in order. Not only was everything in place, he also instructed the house photographer to begin taking candid pictures throughout the evening. And he called in the violinist to accompany the harpist. In his mind, Eric had just doubled Vincent's tip. Cynthia came back looking radiant. While she was in the bathroom she got a chance to check out the ring. She couldn't believe it. It was the same ring as before, which she already loved but with an upgrade, a two-carat center diamond that sparkled as a diamond should. She was so happy.

The waiter greeted them and ushered them to their favorite table. Cynthia noticed the music seemed to get louder with each step they took. "Oh, Eric, that music is just heavenly, isn't it?"

"Yes, it is, but not as heavenly as you." As they turned the corner, Cynthia could see the table, the musicians, and the waiter positioned to pour the champagne. The photographer stayed in the background taking candid shots. Cynthia didn't even notice him. Eric pulled out the chair for his blushing bride to be and handed her the rose. The champagne was poured, and with the music serenading them, they raised their glasses. Cynthia went first, "I love you, Eric." The champagne flutes clicked, they sipped and were raised again. "I love you more, Cyn."

After a wonderful dinner and a whole evening of staring into each other's eyes, they headed for the lounge that featured live music and had a dance floor. They both loved to dance. And whenever they danced together in public, all eyes were on them. Eric gave the cue and the band began to play their favorite love song. One of the band members announced their engagement and called Eric and Cynthia to the dance floor. Everyone clapped as they came to the floor. They danced, and as always, everyone else moved back and watched. Eric held Cynthia in his arms and made a request. He asked Cynthia to close her eyes and keep them closed until the song ended. Cynthia thought it was strange request but she closed her eyes, no questions asked. He held her so tightly as they danced. She felt secure in his strong embrace, and she trusted him to lead her. Eric tenderly kissed her neck and began to whisper in her ear, "While I was in Maui, standing outside my balcony looking at the beautiful sunset, I felt something was missing. All I thought about was you and how I wanted you there to share it with me. And that's when I knew that I wanted to bring you to Maui . . . as my wife. Would you like to honeymoon in Maui, my love?"

Cynthia didn't answer; she was speechless. Cradled in the strong arms of her soon-to-be husband, she cherished every second. This was the place she had always long to be. She could feel Eric's love for her like never before. As the song was ending, Eric lovingly kissed her and told her she could opened her eyes, and when she did Cynthia was stunned, she could not move, she could not talk. Eric laughed and thanked Robbie for coordinating the whole event. They were surrounded with friends and coworkers who were thrilled to share in the celebration. Laurie ran up to Cynthia and bragged on her matchmaking skills, and how she just had a feeling that the two of them would hit it off. Brenda and her husband Dwayne were there, and of course Michael was there but Denise was at home with the new baby. Lawrence, the math genius from his job, was there with his girlfriend Juanita. Even LaDonna, the sales girl at Nordstrom's, showed up with her husband Demetrist. Eric's mother Diane was so happy to meet Cynthia. India assured them that she would always pray for them. Eric even invited Robert and his wife. They came and were very glad to be there. Robert still got under Eric's skin, and probably always would, but Eric learned how to navigate positively through both his and Robert's quirks. The real miracle was not that Eric got along better with Robert, it was the fact that Eric could admit his own quirkiness.

All of her life, Cynthia imagined how she wanted to be proposed to. This was more than she could ever ask or think. Eric had swept Cynthia off her feet, and she had no problem letting him know that he was the man, her man.

# Chapter 30

On Monday morning, fifteen minutes before Eric and Cynthia were to arrive, coach was reviewing her notes from all of their sessions. Both of them had made such tremendous progress in their individual sessions. Coach knew without a shadow of a doubt that they were going to be a completely different couple than when she first met them. This time she didn't expect any arguing, eye rolling, blaming, loud voices, snide remarks, or sarcastic jokes.

Just then, the office door opened and Eric and Cynthia walked in, holding hands and laughing.

COACH: Come on in, you two. You both look so happy, what's going on?

*Cynthia flashed her left hand before me with sheer joy on her face.*

COACH: Wow, what a beautiful ring!

CYNTHIA: Eric proposed! And the way he proposed was so romantic. He outdid himself. It was like a dream come true. I'm so happy.

*Cynthia gave Eric a kiss on the cheek, and he beamed with pride.*

ERIC: I enjoyed planning every detail. It truly was a special night, and I got a whole lot of xoxoxo.

COACH: Cynthia, maybe we can have lunch next week so you can give me all the details.

CYNTHIA: I would love to.

COACH: Have you set a date?

CYNTHIA: Yes, we have. June 19. My parents got married on that day. And since they are no longer with me, I wanted to honor them by getting married on their special day.

COACH: That is so special. I'm sure your parents will be there, smiling down from heaven.

CYNTHIA: Thank you so much, Coach. If it had not been for our sessions with you, we would have never made it to the altar.

ERIC: Amen to that.

COACH: I am so thankful to see the transformation in both of you.

ERIC: You were right. We both had faults that needed to be addressed. Who would have thought that I, Mr. Sarcasm, would ever admit to my own stuff? Now we're relating to each other so much better than we did before. When we first came to you, we argued on the way to the session, during the session, and on the way home from the session. That's what we were laughing about as we walked in. But now, we're walking in to our last session, laughing.

CYNTHIA: Coach, Eric has another praise report to tell you. Go ahead, Eric, tell her.

ERIC: Yes, it's pretty amazing. Just before I left work today my supervisor Robert called me into his office for an urgent private meeting. I had no idea what the urgency was all about. I came into his office, trying to remember all of my newly acquired anger management skills just in case. When I got to his office suite, I was surprised to see the regional supervisor in Robert's office. I sat down and wondered what was really going on. I could not think of any recent incidents that would warrant a reprimand from Mr. Randle. Robert started off by thanking me for inviting him to our engagement party, and how much he and his wife enjoyed themselves. And then he dropped the bomb on me.

Robert's wife had accepted an appointment to become a professor at a UCLA. Robert and his wife were moving to California. Mr. Randle came to inform Robert that his transfer request had had been approved and the company in Los Angeles was looking forward to him being there. I just sat there stunned. From that point, Mr. Randle took over. He complimented me on closing the deal from an investor that the company had been wooing for years. He also told me that all my coworkers told him of the tremendous change that they saw in me and spoke highly of my leadership as project manager. He complimented me and wanted to know if I would be interested in taking over Robert's position. Of course, I said yes. I couldn't believe that the position that I had tried so hard to get for the last three years was handed to me.

COACH: Congratulations, Eric, that's incredible!

CYNTHIA: Only God can do something like that. We are just amazed at how he works.

ERIC: The old mothers at my church growing up always said that the Lord works in mysterious ways. I used to laugh at their old folk sayings, but now I know exactly what they were talking about.

COACH: I'm so happy and proud of the spiritual and emotional growth in you both. I really want to commend you for dealing with the problematic issues in your relationship before getting married. Marriage does not fix personal, psychological, or emotional problems. If anything, marriage will only make matters worse. So many people ignore the red flags and get married anyway. It's no wonder the divorce rate is so high.

CYNTHIA: I think this kind of counseling should be a mandatory requirement for getting a marriage license.

ERIC: Yea, you have to study and be tested for any other kind of license. They should also have mandatory ongoing parenting classes as well.

COACH: Now that's a good point. The divorce rate in America is around 41 percent, and in many cases, irreconcilable difference was cited as the only ground for divorce. And if one party doesn't want the marriage to end, there's little they can do to stop the divorce proceedings. It is extremely easy to dissolve a marriage. If the grounds for divorce are irreconcilable differences, the judge doesn't bother to ask what the differences actually are. What really bothers me is those irreconcilable differences have very little to do with clashing opinions or incompatibility. The irreconcilability issues, for the most part, can be traced to the brokenness found deep within the core of one's own personhood. When these things are not dealt with, couples continue to add more injury to those internal bruises, and that's when the irreconcilable differences start to congeal. God would much rather have you be instrument of healing to each rather than sparring partners.

If couples are able to reconcile their own individual issues, the marriage has a better chance of surviving.

CYNTHIA: I see your point. At our first session, Eric and I were stuck blaming each other for the problems in our relationship, when actually we both had our own irreconcilable issues to deal with.

ERIC: The divorce rate would significantly decrease if couples understood this.

COACH: Yes, it would. I am so glad that you and Cynthia took the time to work on yourselves before walking down the aisle. That is so commendable, and because of your courage and persistence in working on yourselves I can now say "amen" to this union.

CYNTHIA: Yes, I'm glad we did too. I don't want our marriage to end up making the divorce statistics higher than it already is.

ERIC: Not only that, but we have a better chance of having a happy marriage. I know a whole lot of unhappy married people.

COACH: Exactly, no marriage has the "happily ever after" guarantee. I want you both to promise me and each other that when you run into future impasses as husband and wife, it means that it's time for more healing, wisdom, guidance, and instruction. Don't just throw in the towel, work it out.

ERIC: Don't worry, Coach. I already have your number on speed dial. Cynthia had to drag me to the first session, but I will be a willing participant from now on. I promise that if we get stuck, we will call.

CYNTHIA: Okay, Eric, I'm going to hold you to that.

ERIC: I already know you will. You don't forget anything I say, whether good or bad. I don't know how women do that.

COACH: I am so impressed that you both were able to resolve some core issues within yourselves before getting married. If you hadn't, the relationship would have never bonded on the deepest level.

Now for our last time together, I'd like to go summarize the core issues.

For you, Cynthia, when your relationship with your father was suddenly severed, it wasn't intentional on his part, but nonetheless, emotionally you felt abandoned . That deep sense of emptiness and loneliness that you described was coming from that subconscious bruise. Finding love was an urgent and dire need to repair that breach. On top of that, the violence you saw in your home caused you to feel unsafe, insecure, fearful, and anxious. These emotions were the foundational makeup of your soul.

And when Eric charmed his way into your heart, you were hoping that he was the one who would lovingly tend to your needs, but you had no idea how deep those needs really were. Can you see how it would be unfair of you to think that Eric could fulfill those emotional needs?

Cynthia: Yes, I can clearly see that now. There is no way Eric, or any other person for that matter, could touch those deep places.

COACH: Yes, and also, Eric had his own core issues to deal with. In his childhood history, Eric was overwhelmed by his mother's emotional neediness. At an early age, he became his mom's surrogate man. He felt smothered by her love and would withdraw whenever his mother started to get clingy. When the emotional, needy little girl Cynthia would manifest from time to time. And when she did, a subliminal association with his mother's emotional neediest propelled Eric to vanish without an explanation. When Eric disappeared, the original father wound was reinforced as Cynthia felt emotionally abandoned yet again. She had no idea that hidden deep within her "Prince Charming" was a little boy who pulled away from his mother's suffocating hugs. Eric had perfected this escape routine from emotionally smothering females long before he met you, Cynthia.

Eric, you also had an abandonment wound of your own. For years, you felt rejection from your absent father. In addition, the continual broken promises from your dad left an unseen venom of disappointment in your soul. And when you stopped going to church with your mother, you literally felt that you were a disappointment. Now as an adult, the emotional pain of a disappointed little boy who felt rejected shows up in sarcastic, cynical, and arrogant remarks. No one would ever suspect that underneath that vibrant personality was a very sensitive, intelligent child who felt invisible to those who mattered the most, his parents.

With these deeply rooted emotional dynamics firmly in place, both of you were unsuspectingly sabotaging your relationship. Getting married without dealing with your individual dysfunctional patterns, a divorce would have been inevitable. Eric and Cynthia listened intently at coach's every word. They were fascinated how she was able to tie all those emotional loose ends together. And they loved the way she could explain such complex matters in simple terms.

ERIC: That's pretty deep. Who would have guessed we had all of that drama going on inside us.

CYNTHIA: Yeah, we're pretty complex emotional creatures, aren't we?

COACH: Yes, we are. Only God knows what's hidden within the recesses of our heart, mind, and soul. He knows how and when the internal faults were formed. He understands that our behavior is often reflecting our brokenness. While humanity judges our behavior, God looks beyond our external faults and sees the internal maladies of a shattered soul in need of healing. Jesus, the Messiah, made the ultimate sacrifice through his life and death that gave us the incredible gift of salvation. We are not only forgiven for our sins, we are also cleansed, healed, and delivered from its damaging effects.

As we deepen our intimate relationship with the Father, the Holy Spirit will guide us to the truth concerning those dysfunctional places in us, and by the power of his steadfast love and compassion toward us, we are rescued from the debris of emotional pain and despair. Being healed from emotional scars involves uprooting deeply embedded subconscious lies, breaking the powerful subliminal associations from the original wounding experience, and the pulling down of highly exalted false belief systems that have fed and cultivated our dysfunction. If we are willing to go through the process of being made whole, there will be pain as God releases us from the our character flaws and defects, but there will also be great unanticipated, unspeakable joy as we are divinely perfected in and by the love of God. We are consistently being transformed into the person God already declared us to be. It takes time, and it's not a onetime process, but in time we are able to see that we have been made anew.

CYNTHIA: That is so true. I have had to get acquainted with the new me since going through this process.

ERIC: Yea, me too. I had to laugh as I left Robert's office after being offered his position.

On the day of his promotion, Robert was given the traditional "I'm the Boss Now" coffee mug, and as I looked at it on his desk, I remembered all the times I wanted to throw that mug against the wall. And now I'm about receive my very own customary "I'm the Boss Now" coffee mug. God is just too much. I love how he works things out.

CYNTHIA: Oh, Coach, thank you so much for helping Eric and I to reestablish our spiritual connection with God. How in the world can we really live without God's love, mercy, compassion, wisdom, guidance . . . I could go on and on.

COACH: Yes, God loves us so deeply, and when you finally realize that love every day, life becomes full of joy, wonder, and divine favor. Having an intimate relationship with God does have awesome daily benefits. The love of God is just amazing and makes life worth living.

ERIC: I like to describe God's love as: Love with no damaging emotional strings attached.

COACH: Yes, I love how you put it. I'll have to remember that line.

ERIC: Well, to me you have yet to live, if you haven't walked with God in the garden during your short time here on earth. But you know, I also appreciate learning how to pray short prayers. Cynthia and I always talk about those powerful prayers.

CYNTHIA: Oh, Eric, without God's intervention we were headed down a road of disaster. I'm so glad we waited to get married.

ERIC: Yes, our relationship is tight and much better than before.

COACH: God has reconciled those tender, young wounded places to himself, and healed the emotional damage in both of you. He has supernaturally leveled the playing field emotionally so that you can now give and receive pure love to each other.

When you came to your first session, I knew it would be a long journey of healing, and now here we are celebrating all that God has done. Great work guys. I am so proud of both of you.

CYNTHIA: Thank you, Coach . . . thank you so much. We cannot thank you enough.

COACH: You are so welcome. It was an honor for me to witness your individual transformations. I can't wait until June 19.

ERIC: I can't wait either . . . and I can't believe that I'm saying that I can't wait to get married, and I actually mean it.

COACH: Well, let's thank the Lord for what he has done.

*Eric, Cynthia, and coach held hands and prayed. Each of them took turns giving honor to the Lord who looks beyond our faults and sees that our real need is to be made whole. And without condemnation progressively heals us by the supernatural power of his divine love. The presence of the Lord was also there; they were standing on holy ground. After the prayer, they hugged one another and cried. And yes, even the once well-guarded, I'm not going to let you tear down my thick protective emotional walls, Eric wasn't at all ashamed of his tears.*

As they left my office, Eric picked up a bunch of my business cards. "I know plenty of people who need these. Maybe I can get Robert to come in before he leaves . . . and I'm not being sarcastic." Eric asked for me to pray for him. His father was just released from prison after eighteen years. Eric wanted to see him; I assured him that I would.

I tried to prepare for my next session, but all I could think about was what I was going to wear to the wedding and if any eligible men would be attending. Maybe Eric has an uncle . . . Okay, I'm getting too excited, but I know June 19 is going to be a special day for sure.

# Chapter 31

According to my aunt, my father was released from prison last month. My father has been in and out of prison for most of my life. He was never good at life in the real world. With a felony on his record, it was hard for him to get a job, and without employment it's impossible to rent an apartment. He would return to live with one of his many lady friends and quickly resume his old lifestyle. I already knew the pattern, and if everything goes as I suspect, within two years he would be back on lockdown.

Aunt Karen was the only one in the family who believed that my father would one day get back on his feet. She tried to assure me that this time would be different. Apparently, my father was involved in a reentry program designed to give ex-offenders a fresh start so they could focus on rebuilding their lives. The men are given transitional housing, vocational training, and support groups that help with those who struggled with addiction. I was impressed. I hope my father will take full advantage of this opportunity. "Eric, your father has a job!" Aunt Karen was so optimistic. "He was chosen to be part of a work release program. I'm telling you, mark my words, this time is going to be different. He has every component he needs to get it together this time. He's working at a neighborhood grocery store near the transitional house. You should go by and see him. I have the address, here's the card." I unenthusiastically took the card, kissed my aunt, and didn't say whether I was going or not.

Whenever my father got out of prison, I was the one who always made the first move to see him. I was the child, and he was the adult. Why was it my responsibility to reconnect? The last time I talked to him was the day after my high school graduation. He did called from jail. That was different for him. He congratulated me and explained that he got pulled over for speeding and because of several outstanding warrants in several states; he got locked up.

I want to see my father; no let me be real. I want him to see me. I want him to see me now, as a man rather than a starry-eyed kid delighted to be in his presence. I want him to know that I made it without him. I want him to see who's "the man" now. I want him to see my shoes, my clothes, and my car. The tables had turned, and I was going to rub it in his face. I could feel the anger rising. I thought of all kinds of sarcastic remarks, especially for this occasion. As I was parking the car, I realized that I could feel the anger rising. In the past ,there was no internal signal pulling in my reins. I could never feel the anger creeping up; I just got *mad*!

Eric sat in the car for about fifteen minutes; he couldn't move. He had been arrested by the Holy Spirit. As coach would say, more truth was about to be revealed. He began to see his own arrogance and pride. All the "I" statements were self-centered, vindictive, arrogant, and prideful. People were always pointing out his negative attitude and impatience with others, but he could never see it. But as examined his motives for seeing his father, he could see what everyone was talking about. It was crystal clear, he had to acknowledge the log in his own eye. He considered what he would have done to his father without God's grace intervening in his life. He was sure that he would have hit his father as soon as he saw him. Just one good blow to the jaw would have made his day. But now, all he could think about was what God had done in his life. The sessions with the coach, hooking back up with his best friend and his reconnection with his mom. He even saw the anger management class as a blessing. Without it he would have never gotten his promotion. And to top it all off, he was marrying an amazing woman.He asked the Lord to forgive him. "Holy Spirit, thank you for showing me my sin of pride, arrogance, and judgment of my father. Thank you for arresting my negative thoughts and intentions. Thank you for reminding me of all the favor and goodness you have so graciously poured into my life. I wouldn't dare take the credit, all the glory goes to you . . . not me. You have forgiven me and gave me a new life. I ask that you help me do the same for my father. Help me forgive and truly pray for his life to be restored. Who knows maybe one day I will be able to lead him to you, you're always up to something. I never know what miracle you have up your sleeve."

Eric finally got out of the car, and as soon as he walked in the store, he saw his father from a distance. Sure enough, he was stocking shelves. His father couldn't see him, but Eric was watching his every move. His jeans were dirty, his shoes were ragged, and his outfit was a far cry from what he used to wear. He used to get a haircut faithfully every week, and now his hair was a mess. He used to carry around one-hundred-dollar bills, like they were dollars, now he looked like a vagrant. He looked so much older; Eric hoped he was much wiser. Eric was standing directly in back of his father. He wasn't sure what to do next. Suddenly one of the cans slipped from his father's hand and landed at Eric's feet.

His father quickly turned and, without looking up, bent down to retrieve the can. Eric stood still. His father stood up right in front of him; they were eye to eye. "Hey, Dad, remember me?" His father looked like he had seen a ghost. He never wanted his son to see him like this.

"Of course, Son, I know who you are. It's been a long time. How are you?" This became the defining moment for Eric. He already decided not to hit him, curse him, or assault him with sarcasm. He wasn't sure if he should shake his hand, give him a hug, or just answer his question. He chose neither; he stood still and looked his father straight in the eye and said nothing. His father dropped his eyes, stared at the floor, and started talking. "I started to write you so many times, but . . . well, I just thought you'd turn out better if I wasn't around. Your mom wrote to me all the time. She told me how you were doing and how proud of you she was. I knew you had a better chance in life without my influence . . . I didn't want you to follow in my footsteps and turn out like me."

*As he was talking, I noticed that he could not look me in the eye. My pimped out, hotshot dad could not look me in the eye. He didn't straight out apologize, but I could see the guilt and shame he was carrying. I think the only reason I could see it was because I had just been delivered from the same thing, guilt and shame. I saw my father as I had come to see myself. And for the first time in my life, I actually felt sorry for him. I understood what coach meant when she said that my father was emotionally handicapped; he still is. But I'm not, I'm free. He didn't want me to turn out like him; well, it was unanimous nobody wanted me to turn out like him. God was confirming what he had said to me, and it was better for me to not be with my father . . . that's what God said. I can see that my father did care for me. He cared enough to sacrifice his relationship with me, just to give me a better chance in life.*

"Aunt Karen told me you were working here. I came by to let you know that I'm getting married, and I wanted to give you this." Eric handed him a wedding invitation. His father was eager to accept the invite.

"I thought you would never invite me to anything ever again . . . Okay, Son, I'll be there."

And that was it. Eric said nothing else; he turned and walked out the store. His father went back to work. Eric got in his car and before taking off, he paused to reflect on his thoughts and how he felt about seeing his father. *He said he would be there. Maybe he will, maybe he won't, but either way, I won't be disappointed or angry. God has done way too much for me to act like that. Hum . . . he called me son.* He's never called me son. Eric drove away with another miracle. When he was about thirteen years old, just before he stopped praying to God because his prayers were never answered, Eric asked if his father could one day call him son. This day his prayer was answered. God answered . . . God did it. Eric was overwhelmed. "My heavenly father sure has some smooth moves. I get all excited when I see a good three pointer in a game. Hum, that ain't nothing. God sinks shots executed from years back and sinks the shot. Damn, he's good . . . oh sorry God, I shouldn't have said it quite like that, forgive me. Let me rephrase, Lord there is none like you. You deserve all of the glory, both now and forever more."

# Chapter 32

On the morning of June 19, her wedding day, Cynthia had mixed emotions. Her parents were married on that day, and although she was happy about being married to the love of her life, she missed her parents. She picked up the wedding photo of her parents from the fireplace mantle. She held it close to her heart, kissed both parents, and thought about their marriage. Yes, they did have tumultuous times, but yet they stayed together, and it wasn't just for the sake of the children. As she got older, Cynthia began to see that her parents really did love each other, in their own way. They had that 'till death do us part' kind of marriage. God honored their commitment, and her father conquered his alcohol addiction, the fighting stopped, and her parents started enjoying each other again. They would take regular trips to Las Vegas and always had a great time. Cynthia called her mother "Ms. Lady Luck" because she always had lucky streaks on the slot machines. Her father would stay close to her mom just to stand watch over her winnings. Cynthia laughed as she remembered her mother trying to sneak away from her father so she wouldn't have to share her money.

Cynthia would never forget the last conversation she had with her mother as she laid in the hospital bed dying. Her mother told her that she enjoyed her life with her children, and she wanted them to always remember the fun they had. "Didn't we have a ball, we had fun, didn't we? Try to think about those times. And whatever you do make sure you stay close to your brothers and sister, and most importantly always stay close to God. Don't forget, Cynthia, we know *somebody!*" The "somebody" she was referring to was God.

After her mother died, Cynthia's father moved in with her older brother. She would visit often and share some wonderful moments with her father.

She treasured every moment with him. During the last five years of his life, Cynthia felt like his special girl again. From the time she was six years old, she prayed that her father would stop drinking and that they would be close again. It took a long time for that prayer to be answered, but it was. Cynthia was very grateful for the time she had with her father before he passed away. While cleaning out the drawers in his room after her father died, Cynthia found her Cinderella watch that she had gotten for Christmas when she was six years old. It was her very first watch, and her father had kept it all these years. After finding the watch, Cynthia knew that her father never stopped loving her even though he was wrestling with his own demons.

With tears in her eyes, she said happy anniversary to her parents, kissed the picture again, placed it back on the mantel, and headed upstairs to get ready for her wedding.

§

The first thing that Eric saw when he opened his eyes was his tuxedo hanging on the closet door. He laughed. "Yea, God's got jokes. It's like I was positioned exactly to see the tux first thing. Yes, I'm getting married today. Me, the one who said . . . I'll never get married, why we do have to get a piece of paper to prove that we love each other, why can't we just live together like everyone else? I'm getting married . . . and I'm happy about it. God truly is a miracle worker."

§

When I entered the church, I felt like I had entered the Garden of Eden. Flowers were everywhere and the fragrance of roses filled the air. I was captivated by the beauty, and when the usher came to take me to my seat, I was caught off guard. He asked my name, and when I turned to answer, I was startled; he was so handsome. When I was finally able to speak, I told him my name. "Oh, you're the coach that Eric and Cynthia always talk about. They told me to look out for you. You have a special seat reserved in the front. I would be honored to escort you." I tried to keep my composure as he locked my arm in his and walked me to the front of the church. I thanked him as I took my seat.

When Eric walked out with the minister and his best man, I smiled. He didn't look nervous at all. But I noticed that he was looking around the audience. Then it dawned on me, he was looking for his dad. All I could think was Jesus please let him be here. I saw Eric smiling and nodding his head like he was acknowledging someone. Then, his gaze turned to me. He was trying to tell me something. Oh . . . his dad is sitting right front of me. Thank you, Jesus!

Cynthia came down the aisle to a violin and harp duet. She was *gorgeous!* Ms. Glamour Girl was far more exquisite than that ring on her finger. Ms. Diva outdid herself, that's Cynthia. I wouldn't expect anything less. As they lovingly said their vows, they looked like celebrities. And when the minister introduced them as husband and wife, I cried tears of joy. God did it; it was his healing love that prepared them for this day, and watching them unite in holy matrimony was such a witness to me of God's faithfulness.

The reception was just as fabulous as the wedding. Everything . . . the food, music, décor, and the cake, just fabulous! Michael stood to give a toast to the newlyweds, "Here's to the bride. May you share everything with your husband . . . and that includes the housework. Eric, please take Cynthia's hand and place your hand over hers. Now, Eric, I want you to remember this moment and cherish it . . . because this will be the last time you'll ever have the upper hand!" Everyone laughed, especially those who were married.

"Seriously I am honored to be Eric's best man. I have known Eric since college, and I honestly thought I would never see this day. I am so happy for the both of you. May you be friends to each other as only lovers can. And may you love each other as only best friends can. Always keep God at the center of your relationship, be quick to forgive each other because a marriage cannot be sustained without forgiveness. Lastly, keep in mind that a successful marriage requires falling in love many times, always with the same person. Our blessings are with you. May the Lord give you a love affair for life. Everyone clicked their glasses and cheered. Eric and

Cynthia danced the first dance. They embraced each other so lovingly; it was obvious that they cherished each other.

When the master of ceremonies announced that it was time for the bridal toss, I noticed that not one of the single women got up to catch the bridal bouquet. That was always the case when it came to the men catching the bride's garter belt, but it was highly unusual for the single women to remained seated. Usually, the floor is crowded with women willing to leap into the air like a basketball player at the beginning jump shot of the game. Motivated by the hopes of being the next bride to walk down the aisle, they positioned themselves and was ready to wrestle down any opponent. I looked at the faces of the women and saw looks of despair. Heads were shaking in a "no way" fashion as if to say "no, really I'm good. I don't have to be married." And then I thought to myself, I'm single, but I wasn't getting up either. I had been married at one time, but my marriage ended about seven years ago. On the day that my divorce was finalized, I walked out of the courtroom making a declaration that I would never get married again. I was so disillusioned by the whole concept of being in love, and just the thought of marriage brought shivers to my spine.

Like Cynthia, I had desperately searched for love and only found disappointment. And like Eric, I made sarcastic remarks whenever I talked about being married. As I counseled them, I became conscious of the fact that I needed healing myself. I bowed my head for a brief moment and prayed, "Father God, I come to you with my own wounded places. Please heal me from the residue of disappointment. I know that you have ordained marriage, and I need your help so that I would once again believe in love. If marriage is in your plan for my life, heal me and let your will be done. Amen."

After my prayer, I decided to join the single women for the toss. And when Cynthia threw the bouquet, I caught it. It was easy, like it was simply handed to me. And what shocked me the most was I received the bouquet with no fear or anxious thoughts, no mocking or sarcastic comments, and without a single trace of desperation wondering who and when I would marry.

Eric and Cynthia walked over and congratulated me on catching the bouquet. They were so excited for me.

"Coach, it is not good for you to be alone."

"Yeah, Coach, just like my husband said. We pray for you all the time. Don't you want to get married?"

*The question caught me off guard, and I couldn't answer right away. Little did they know that they weren't the only ones being healed during their sessions. As I was coaching them, God was also touching my spirit and watching their relationship grow gave me hope to believe in love again.*

"Yes, Cynthia, I do."

"Great. I want to introduce you to someone."

*She motioned for someone to come to the table. I almost fell out of my seat. It was the extremely good-looking man who escorted me to my seat.*

ERIC: Coach, I'd like to introduce you to my favorite uncle.

*All I could say to myself was* "Thank you, Jesus!"

# Everlasting Love

God's Love is so amazing.
We can't ever really fathom it.
Even in all we know
We could never imagine a love so wonderful and powerful.

You don't have to earn it.
You just have to receive it.
And there's no threat of ever losing it.
He'll never withdraw it, no matter what happens.
His love will always see you through.

This is an ever blossoming, intimate relationship between God and you,

That is destined to be
a
Love affair for life.


**God Is Love**
**1 John 4:8**

# Addendum

This novel was written with you in mind

## A Love Affair for Life

## Healing Workbook

ೋౘ

*Here is your opportunity to be healed. Do You Want to Be Made Whole?*

ೋౘ

## In this section you will find:

- Coach's reflections and notes on sessions.
- Questions for you to answer and think about.
- Emotional chart given to Cynthia—Chapter 3.
- Exercises that were given to Eric and Cynthia for you to complete.
- Illustrations.
- Scriptures.

# Guidelines for Your Journey

Each chapter of the book contains wisdom for you to apply to your life.
Expect to be transformed by the power of God's love

•**Keep your Bible handy**—Cynthia didn't know where her Bible was. Do you have a Bible? Do you know where it is? When was the last time you read it?

•**When doing the assignments**—make sure you won't be interrupted. Turn off the phone and tell the family you need a time out.

•**Keep a journal**—write down your observations, revelations, and answers to the exercise questions. Your journal will serve as a memorial of your personal journey to wholeness.

•**Pray**—Prayer is an essential tool on this journey. Even simple prayers have power. Talk to God like he's right there in the room (because he is). He's just a prayer away.

•**Be open and honest**—Emotional healing requires facing facts head-on, no matter how unpleasant. It's important that you open yourself up and trust the process.

•**Don't block your emotional and spiritual growth**—by blaming or judging others, If you stay in denial you will get stuck. You may not go backwards but you're wasting time not moving forward. No one knows how much time they have, don't waste it.

- **Don't become paralyzed in emotional pain**—This process is not designed to overwhelm you with guilt, shame, fear, or perpetual defeat. If the Lord brings it up, it's time to be healed.

- **Referrals**—If you need more support, go to a professional Christian counselor, psychologist, or psychiatrist. If medicine is prescribed, take it.

- **You will get healed as you go**—Commit to the process. Some days will be hard emotionally, but keep going and know that you get healed as you go.

# Chapter 1

**Notes from coach:**

After reading over their paperwork, I could see that both Eric and Cynthia had a lot of emotional work to do. Very few people realize that untreated emotional wounds can sabotage even the best of relationships. They look like a great couple, but they must be committed to the process of healing before they make a lifetime commitment to each other.

Eric resisted going for counseling. Would it be difficult for you to go for counseling?
What is the most intimate relationship you have? What is it like?
Do you argue all the time or do you never have arguments?
How do you argue?
When you have disagreements are you able to resolve them?
Eric and Cynthia blamed each other for their relationship issues. Do you constantly blame your partner for the problems in your relationship?
Are you in denial about your role in the equation? Or do you accept all the blame when there's a problem in the relationship?

# Chapter 2

Eric was driving fast just to get on Cynthia's nerves. Do you do things just to irritate your partner?
Eric called Cynthia a "drama queen." Are you overly dramatic, over the top, and exaggerated while trying to resolve a relationship issues?
Do you act like nothing-ever-bothers you when it really does?
Are you a martyr walking around carrying everybody's pain while neglecting your own emotional issues?
Cynthia had to take control at all times. Does that sound like you? Do you fight to get and keep the upper hand in your relationship?
Do you have a tendency to make mountains out of molehills when it comes to problems in your relationship . . . or are you ignoring elephants in the room?
What kind of avoidances tactics do you use? . . . Or are you chomping at the bit to immediately confront offensives?

When you and your partner come back together after a blow up, is the issue that started the problem swept under the rug or do you pick the argument back up . . . in a few days?

## Chapter 3

Cynthia was a pro at skirting over things she didn't want to address. Are you good at that as well?

Coach felt Cynthia was an overachiever. How would you describe yourself? Overachiever/perfectionist/underachiever.

What's the real motive behind your purpose-driven life?

Cynthia felt that being married would somehow complete her. Are you waiting for something or someone to come into your life to complete you?

§

*If you are unhappy and single, you'll probably be unhappy when you get married. Marriage does not fix spiritual, personal, psychological, or emotional problems. If anything, marriage will exacerbate them.*

*If you are not happy with yourself and your life, take responsibility to fix it now while you are single. Your future spouse will thank you.*

Cynthia talked about a deep pain trapped inside of her that surfaced when she felt lonely.

Do you have a deep emotional pain that feels familiar and have just learned to live with it?

Cynthia wasn't sure how she really felt most of the time. Coach had to show her a chart of different emotions to help her become more in touch with herself.

Here's the chart. Perhaps it will help you.

## Chapter 4

Cynthia went shopping to alleviate her emotional distress. What diversions do you use to avoid emotional pain? Cynthia wasn't sure how she really felt most of the time. Are you in touch with your emotions?

## Chapter 5

Does Cynthia's statement, "If I start crying, I won't stop" resonate with you?
Do you hate being or feeling out of control?
Was there fighting, screaming, physical violence in your home?
Was there sexual, mental, verbal, or substance abuse in your home? Is it time to find a counselor?
Growing up, were you left alone in your sorrows?

## Chapter 6

As a child, did you feel it was your job to keep either of your parents happy?
Do you have any unresolved issues with your mother/father/or anyone else?
Do you need emotional healing? This is a trick question; we all need emotional healing.
Do you have a Bible? Cynthia didn't know where her Bible was? Where is yours?
You'll need it for your first assignment.

### Assignment 1
Instructions:

Make sure you will not be disturbed for at least thirty minutes.
Pray before, during, and after your time in the Word.
Slowly Read Psalm 23 every day *for one week*.
Keep a journal of your thoughts as you read. Underline words that seem to catch your eye . . . meditate on that one particular thought for a whole day. Focus on another part of the scripture each day.

## Chapter 7

Eric had no problem showing his anger. How do you handle anger?
If you are currently in a relationship, do you feel obligated to get married?
Or are you the one putting the pressure on to get married?

## Chapter 8

Cynthia was okay until "that song" came on.
Is there a song that conjures up a strong negative emotional response in you?

## Chapter 9

**Notes from coach:**

During the session something significant emerged. The impression was so deep that Cynthia literally yelled out . . . *Who's going to love me now?* There it was, the epiphany, the moment of enlightenment. This statement had nothing to do with her recent breakup with Eric.
She had just discovered an abandoned part of herself that contained the beginning notes of the now apparent theme song of her life.
It was a desperate cry that came from a deep distant place, a forgotten place, an abandoned place. It came from the core of a broken and bruised heart formed during childhood.
Like a trigger, this melody signaled that it was time to find someone else to love her. As the song played subconsciously within,

We all have subliminal melodies chanting the sentiments of subconscious breaches within. There are behavioral patterns attached to the echoing cries of the brokenness of our personhood.

Cynthia would go from relationship to relationship only to be abandoned again and again.

Instead of suppressing and ignoring her statement, she must pay attention to that desperate cry. She needs a new song.

I pray that she is ready to let God in . . . He wants access to that place. If she surrenders the pain to him, she will be healed.

> Were you involved in romantic relationships as a child?
> Do you always have to be in a relationship?
> Are you afraid to commit to a relationship?
> Can you identify with the empty and lonely feelings Cynthia described?
> How far do these feelings go back? What are they connected to?

Can you identify your subconscious theme song?

It's a repetitive phrase that you find yourself subtly saying to yourself.

It may start out as a conversation you're having with yourself about yourself, or a situation.

It usually centers on what's wrong with you.

A hint of desperation is often there. Sarcasm or apathy may be present as well.

It can be a panicky song or a faint desperate cry.

### Assignment 2

Write out the subconscious theme of your broken core. Caution, don't wallow in negative pits. Submit everything to God along the way.

# Chapter 10

Over the span of two years, Cynthia had accumulated over a month of personal and sick days.

When was the last time you took a real vacation? Family Reunions Don't count as Vacations.

Are you living a balanced Life?

Psalm 46:10a (NKJV)
Be still and know that I Am God . . .
Psalm 84:4 (NKJV)
Blessed are those who dwell in your house: they will be still praising thee.
Selah

**Assignment 3**

Pray, read slowly, meditate, and write in your Journal.
This is not to be rushed through.

**Be Still and Know**
Part I
**Position yourself in a peaceful, still, quite place. Pray and read.**

Be still people. We are too *busy*, slow down! God wants us to learn how to be still.
According to Psalm 23:2, the Lord leads us beside still waters. Everyone knows the calming effect of a lake or ocean. God has provided in nature, places that are designed to woo us to relax and commune with him.
God desires to impart peace deep within our souls. More often than not, our souls are filled with, fear, worry, anxiety, and stress.
Relaxation is vital for soul restoration. Being still puts us in a frame of mind that is conducive for reflection and meditation on the one who is higher than I.
This is the place where you come to know with confidence that he is God, and you are not. In stillness we are positioned to hear his still, small voice guiding us. We may receive an impartation of wisdom, comfort, or revelation.
We are God's workmanship. As you submit your soul issues to his care, God is busy at work transforming
you from the inside out. He is restoring your soul with his healing grace. It's amazing what a rested, well-nurtured, spirit-refreshed soul can endure, create, and accomplish.
As you behold him, you will be changed in divine increments, from glory to glory.

## Be Still and Know
## Part II
**Position yourself in a peaceful still, quiet place**
**Read the following out—loud and very slowly.**

I am more than just a higher power. Why have a spirit guide when you can have me, the Almighty God—up close and personal. I am calling and drawing you closer to me.

I am not too big or too busy for you. I am not a distant ruler reigning in some distant heaven. I am *not* so preoccupied with the big issues of the world that I don't care about you.

I never have and never will forget or abandon you.

Nor am I angry with you. You may be mad at me for allowing certain things to happen in your life. All I can say for now is that I will overshadow the pain you have experienced. I know how to turn ashes to beauty if you would just trust me. You may never fully understand some of the situations that occurred in your life, but I do.

I ask that you learn to trust me. I know it may be difficult for you to do that, but I am wooing you back to me—gently, gingerly, and most assuredly.

I want to be intimately connected to you so that I can nurture you with a love like none you've ever known—safe and gentle, patient and forgiving, protecting and defending.

I have a plan for your life, and as my plan unfolds, you will realize that you have great purpose and significant contributions to make while you are on this earth.

When I lead you to difficult places, those that have caused you deep pain, be confident in me. I will release my power to heal, reconstruct, and realign you. I want to encourage, affirm, and empower you. I am grooming you for your unique greatness and guiding you in the direction of your destiny.

I'm so glad you're inviting me to be more intimate with you. I will teach you how to recognize my voice and receive my love. I will also teach you about yourself.

Only I know you completely. You have seen only glimpses of who I created you to be.

I am preparing you on purpose for your purpose, my purpose. As you abide in me, I will reveal truths to you that will set you free. Remember that I love you utterly, completely, and unconditionally.

I just need you to *be still and know that I am God.*

Did you sense God speaking to you?
Which words touched you the most?
Keep listening . . . Is he still speaking?
If so, write it down in your journal.

**Assignment** 4

**Discovering your anxious places**
**Psalm 139:23-24**
**Pray, read, meditate, pray, read, meditate . . . write.**

ಸುಂಡ

Don't suppress your emotions.
Work through Them with the
Lord.

ಸುಂಡ

What fuels your anxious places?
How has anxiousness led you down the wrong path?
If you feel you have disappointed God, how do you deal with your guilt?
God is not going to leave or abandon you on this journey.
He is perfecting you, bringing you into maturity.

Ask for his wisdom, strength, knowledge, and understanding.

## Chapter 11

Do you use gifts to in as a substitute for true intimacy?
Are you afraid to be in a committed relationship?
Have you felt invisible to others?

## Chapter 12

**Notes from coach:**

From this session we see the root problem. Cynthia's self-image was shattered to the core. Her father traded her quality time with him with liquor.
A breach had now formed in the depths of her tender psyche realigning her soul from an inner place of security to a place of abandonment.
Although her father remained in the home, he was no longer emotionally present in her life.
He had unknowingly forsaken his daughter as he medicated his own emotional pain with alcohol.
Cynthia internalized the disruptive breach into the core her own emotional makeup.

---

**Keep Going**

**Dealing with emotional issues from the past can be exhausting. But do not become paralyzed in emotional despair**

**God doesn't want your painful past to block your abundantly blessed future. Keep going. You will get healed as you go.**

*Psalm 27:10 (NKJV)*
*When my mother and my father forsake me then the Lord will take care of me.*

Notice that the scripture says (when) they forsake you, not (if) they forsake you.

As Cynthia got closer to the root of her pain, before she could really feel it, she called Eric for comfort. It was a knee jerk reaction.
When you feel emotional pain, do you have a knee jerk reaction?
Who or what do you turn to for comfort?

# Chapter 13

Eric didn't get the job and was extremely upset about it.
Are you currently dealing with a major disappointment in your life?
How are you dealing with it?

**Notes from coach:**

At the beginning of our session, Eric was angry about not getting the promotion he felt he deserved. He was offended when it was suggested that he go to anger management classes. And although everyone, including myself could see his arrogance and sarcasm, he would not even entertain the thought that these observations from others had any truth to them.
He used sarcasm as a barrier to block others from getting to know the real Eric. In his session, he did admit that he had sarcastic tendencies, so he is not completely oblivious. Humility was a virtue that Eric certainly needs. He mentioned that he felt invisible because he didn't get the promotion, but I'm sure he felt invisible during childhood.
Remember, we all have themes of brokenness within that manifest in our current situations. Cynthia's unconscious theme was "who's going to love me now?" I suspect that Eric's theme is "who's going to see me now?"

> Every parent has at one time or another unknowingly nicked their child's delicate psyche

## Chapter 14

Were you raised in a strict religious home? How did that affect your relationship with God?
Are you self-confident or arrogant?
Are you typically sarcastic? Why?

## Chapter 15

### Assignment 5
#### How deep is your love for God?
Pray before answering the questions.
Keep the prayer short, simple, and to the point.

---

1. Do you love God?

___ Very much ___ Moderately ___ Sometimes ___ Not at all
___ Haven't really thought about it ___ I did a long time ago

2. Do you sense that God loves you?

___ Very much ___ Moderately ___ Sometimes ___ Not at all
___ Haven't really thought about it ___ I did a long time ago

---

**Check what most applies to you**
**Take some time to think about the boxes you checked.**

**Write out the answers to the following questions:**
**Do you love God?**

**Do you believe God loves you?**

## Chapter 16

Were you used as a bargaining chip by either of your parents?
Be careful single mothers; don't use your son as a surrogate emotional partner. It's damaging for you and your son.

## Chapter 17

At times do you feel like a child trapped in an adult body? You probably need to explore that.

## Chapter 18

**Notes from coach:**

I felt such compassion for Eric as he walked out of my office. As a child, Eric really had star quality. He was a smart, athletic, gifted little boy, but his parents did not affirm him. I call this *affirmation deprivation*. This kind of deprivation for a vulnerable child results in internal impressions that they are less than, not wanted, not loved, or somehow invalid. Without affirmation from parents, it makes it difficult for a child to realize their unique greatness and special qualities. As adults they seek affirmation and devise all kinds of ways to get it. These are the people who feel the need to loudly toot their own horns, hoping someone will pay attention to them. This is the stuff arrogance is made of.
Like Cynthia, Eric went to church as a child, but never developed a relationship with God.
The motive behind Jesus' healing ministry was compassion, and during our time together, I could feel the love of God so strongly.
As I think about his relationship with his parents, I can see why Eric had a hard time committing to an intimate relationship. His mother was using him to soothe her broken heart by making him her emotional caretaker. Be careful moms, don't make this mistake. Your children are not equipped to be your surrogate husband, friend, or companion.

Eric's relationship with his father was definitely a sore spot for him. I could hear his hurt when he talked about trying to buy a Father's Day card for his dad. His father never kept his promises and wasn't around to affirm his manhood. Instead of being a positive role model for his son to embrace, Eric's father became the template for what Eric did not want to become. As a child, Eric longed to be noticed by a father, and now he's still trying to get this need met for affirmation from his career. It is also important to understand that unhealthy relationships with our parents, particularly with the father, often causes complications in how God is perceived. Children learn about God through their parents and so many adults have unknowingly hindered their children from coming to him. There are so many things about God that Eric has yet to learn. This assignment will help him discover new dimensions of God's love, grace, favor, mercy, and kindness toward him. I look forward to our next session.

# Chapter 19

## Assignment 6

**Hearing God's voice and understanding his heart—if only Adam had understood God's heart towards him. Read Genesis, chapter 3.**

In the beginning when God created Adam and Eve, he placed them in a beautiful garden. It was God's desire to fellowship with them as they walked together in the cool of the day. In the beginning, we—the human race—were intimate with God. God intended for this intimate connection to always remain intact. However, after mankind chose to disobey God's one request, something drastic happened. Man suffered a devastating spiritual mutation. Man was no longer able to perceive the true character of God. Subsequently, he lost his own true character. His internal wiring to God was broken and that action inherently changed him. He was no longer connected to his Creator, his very life source.
Man has been faulty ever since.
Adam and Eve hid from God because of fear and shame. Rather than relying on God's solutions for them, they became self-reliant and made fig leaf coverings for their nakedness. In essence, they no longer trusted God to meet their needs.

However, it is imperative to realize that it wasn't God who abandoned man; it was man who abandoned God. God went on a search, looking for the man he had created. God called out to man, "Adam, where are you? Where is the man that I created? Where is the man that enjoyed being in my presence and looked forward to hearing my voice?" God was calling and looking for Adam and Eve, not to punish them but to reestablish the divine, intimate relationship that was lost. Ultimately, the sacrificial death of Jesus, the Messiah, reestablished that connection.

**Insights for your consideration, meditation, and reflection**

God called out to man and said, "Where are you?" God was speaking to them.
Adam could still sense God's presence and heard his voice *after* he disobeyed him. (Gen. 3:8-10).
Man's response to sensing God's presence was to hide from him among the trees of the garden.

> When you sense God's presence, do you want to hide?
> Why?
> What are you hiding among?
> Is God pursuing and calling out to you?
> Are you giving him the silent treatment?

**God wants to be in an intimate relationship with you. Even though you may not feel worthy to be in His presence**

*Even though all of this happened, God didn't abandon, neglect, or ignore man.*
God did address the issues at hand and talked to man concerning his current state and situation.

> *What issues or situations in your life is God trying to address with you?*

The blame game commenced . . . Adam blamed God and Eve for his disobedience. He refused to take responsibility for his choices.

> *Who or what are you blaming for the problems in your life?*
> *It's time to grow up and take responsibility for your actions.*

Eve admits that the serpent deceived her. The real culprit is now identified—the serpent. He came with deception.

*In what ways have you allowed the enemy to deceive you? What has he said to you to make you stay disconnected from an intimate relationship with God?*

God spoke prophetically in Genesis 3:15 concerning the sacrificial death of Jesus, which would reestablish our intimate relationship with God.

## *Our Heavenly Father*

The job of a parent is to protect the vulnerability of their children. Parents have a tremendous responsibility. They must provide wisdom, instruction, guidance, love, provision, nurture, and affirmation in order for their child to grow up with minimal emotional scars. God wants to be that kind of parent to us. He has access to the broken child still alive in you and is able to supernaturally supply the emotional support lacking in your childhood. Although you are an adult, he has access to the wounded child who's still alive in you. You may consider yourself to be all grown up, but he still calls you his child.

Change is often hard and painful, but God makes everything beautiful in his time.

Spend some time writing in your journal.
After doing this exercise, Eric discovered a greater dimension of God's love for him.
What about you?
Has your view of God expanded?

## Chapter 20

**Notes from coach:**

Cynthia's session was very intense. The Holy Spirit began to reveal more truth to Cynthia about her wounded core. God showed her that she had literally abandoned a part of herself. She got a glimpse of this abandoned place when she described how she felt going to the boss's office. Through her session she got a full view of that lost place within herself. God gave her some images that were an accurate reflection of her bruised psyche. As the session continued, she began to realize that the needy part of her personality was in fact the frozen, little abandoned six-year-old-girl Cynthia who was traumatized with fear as she saw her parents fighting. When she got in touch with that part of herself, Cynthia rejected herself. In essence, she was saying "I reject that little girl. I don't even like her." She had no compassion for herself.

As a child, Cynthia was always looking for a hero to rescue her. She didn't know that God would turn out to be that hero. Through his power that was working in her, he brought her face-to-face with the real issue that needed to be addressed. At first, she was unable to forgive herself for being a frighten little girl who couldn't handle the crisis at hand. She didn't realize it, but she had abandoned herself. Jesus was there to empower her as he brought reconciliation to a ruptured place in the core of her personhood. This was a place that no human touch could ever reach. Jesus stood there lovingly, overshadowing and overseeing the whole process of reconciliation as the internal breach was supernaturally healed. With his power, the fault within was realigned from place of extreme paralyzing fear to a place of stability and peace. Cynthia now understands that her deep longing to be loved not only came about because of her severed intimate connect with her father, but it also connected to the fact that she had abandoned a part of herself. It was the wounded child within who was lonely, left alone in a fearful state. Cynthia was made whole by the miraculous power of God.

> How many parts of us are still locked away somewhere in the icy cold deep freezer of childhood trauma?

What are some of your weaknesses, and how do you feel about them?
Do you overplay your strengths to mask your vulnerable self?
Ask God to help you bond with the places you may have rejected and abandoned.

The following illustrations depict what Cynthia described in her session.

# Illustrations

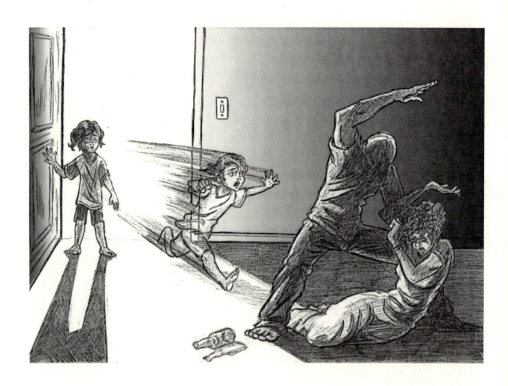

## Chapter 21

Eric vowed to never step foot in another church.
Do you have any inner vows you need to retract?

## Chapter 22

**Notes from coach:**

Eric's mother made some mistakes in raising her son, but what parents didn't? I thought it was very interesting that all this time Eric thought he was a disappointment to his mother, but his mom always thought that she was a disappointment to him. She kept the secret of her own drug addiction from him all these years. Obviously, God has done some tremendous work in her heart for her to have the courage to share that part of her life with Eric. Her confession brought about a connection that she and Eric both needed. Eric's intimacy issues that actually stemmed from the mistakes his mother made was being healed as she revealed truth to him. It was easy for him to forgive her. But forgive his father . . . Hmm, don't know how easy that will be.

## Chapter 23

Cynthia did something special for Eric. When was the last time you surprised your significant other with something very special?

## Chapter 24

Eric was so thankful to coach for the change in his life since going through counseling. He expressed his gratitude by bringing her flowers. Go out and show somebody some love. Who is that special someone you need to show appreciation to?

## Chapter 25

Eric got a chance to spend some time with a friend that was divinely reconnected to his life at the perfect time. Has God ever done that for you? Isn't the sovereignty of God amazing? How does he do that . . . the timing . . . God is so incredibly awesome!

Eric goes off on Robert and as a result is instructed to go to anger management classes. How do you treat your employees, co-workers, or people in your church?

Be mindful to bless others who have been a blessing to you.

## Chapter 26

Eric didn't want to go to the workshop, but he needed it. He would have never moved beyond this point in his life if he didn't deal with his stuff. God even set it up so that Eric had to go. God is always behind the scene helping to get us where we need to go.

**Behaviors that indicate anger issues:**

Giving the silent treatment.

Withholding—sex, affection, or compliments.

Passive-aggressive tendencies.

Constantly putting others down, criticizing, being judgmental, making cynical comments, and sarcastic humor.

Angry people tend to demand things—fairness, appreciation, agreement.

Hurtful childhood events or subconscious memories of traumatic experiences can also trigger anger that is still buried within.

For instance, the tone in which your boss speaks to you may irritate you and feelings of anger begin to slowly emerge.

And yet you have no idea that subconsciously his tone reminds you of your father's tone. The sound of your boss's voice triggers your father issues and you respond . . . as a child.

*Time to Put Away Childish Things And Childish Behaviors*

How well do you think this person will respond if reprimanded by his boss?

The aim is not to suppress anger, but convert it into constructive behavior.

If you have anger issues don't deny it, go get the help you need.

# Chapter 27

**Notes from coach:**

Cynthia has done great in her sessions. She never gave up. Even when it was hard and painful, she was courageous.

- She gained understanding that explained her compulsion to quickly bond emotionally.
- She found the answers as to why the compulsion began, and why she chose to accept any proposed relationship that often led her down the wrong path.
- She recognized that her relationship choices were fueled from a hidden festering wound in her soul.
- She is free from emotional pain—the deep, achy feeling trapped inside—loneliness.

God says in his word that we must be strong and very courageous. Cynthia was just that.

It's not easy to see the brokenness within yourself, but if you want to be made whole, it's imperative that you look back so that you can effectively move forward.

**Take note of any progress you have made on your journey to wholeness.**

Make sure you acknowledge even the incremental changes.

Remember this is not a race to the finish, but a spiritual alignment in your fear, guilt, shame-based soul.

Are you experiencing a paradigm shift in your relationship with God? Has the level of your faith been stretched to capacities you've never experienced? Has your circumstances demanded a change in the way you think about God?

# Chapter 28

Eric makes the big decision . . . Is there a big decision you have to make? Acknowledge God he will direct you.

In all your ways acknowledge him, and he shall direct your paths. Prov.3:6 (KJV)

# Chapter 29

Eric proposes with his whole, transformed, healed heart.

## Chapter 30

The last session with coach.
A time of rejoicing.
Psalm 30:5b (KJV)
. . . weeping may endure for the night, but joy comes in the morning.

## Chapter 31

**Eric visits his father:**

Have you ever considered the emotional wounds of your parents? They were probably victims of their own childhood situations. It is a complicated and complex system of generational issues. What good does it do to judge or blame your parents? We need insight and wisdom to break the complex system of generational curses.
God is able to see the devastation of many generations. He knows your whole family tree, every root and branch on both your mother and father's side. This is God's vantage point. He sees it all, knows it all, and is able to transform you through it all.
You may never know all the answers to perplexing questions, and some things you will never fully understand. But since God knows, this is where trusting him kicks in. Our job is to just surrender our emotional pain to him and forgive our parents; or anyone else.

## Chapte 32

**June 19 celebration:**
Coach's confess that she had her own issues to deal with. She acknowledges her need for healing as well. Those who lead others are also in need of healing. I told you we all need emotional healing. Make sure you deal with your stuff. The world we be a better place if everybody did.

# § Scriptures

Now unto him who is able to do exceeding abundantly above all that we ask or think according to the power that is working in you. Eph. 3:20 (KJV)

. . . being confident of this very thing, that He who has begun a good work in you will complete it until the day of Jesus Christ; Philp.1:6 (NKJ)

Now to Him who is able to keep you from stumbling, And to present you *faultless* Before the presence of His glory with exceeding joy, To the only wise God our Saviour, [be] glory and majesty, dominion and power, both now and ever. Amen. Jude 1:24-25 (NKJV)

Edwards Brothers,Inc!
Thorofare, NJ 08086
19 January, 2011
BA2011019